I0703543

Above Us

By

Victor Liviu Pufulescu

Dedication

I dedicate this book to my father, whose lifelong passion for books and love of reading, inspired and encouraged me to write.

Acknowledgment

I acknowledge Queensland Book Publishers for their professionalism, guidance, and support during the publication of this book.

Table of Contents

Chapter 1:
On An Australian Winter's Night

True Story

The car was rolling silently down the mountain on a narrow and winding road. The engine was running at ease, and inside the cabin, romantic music was playing discreetly in the background.

I had tuned the radio to one of my favourite stations and, surrounded by that tranquil atmosphere, I was just gazing at the dark road. The headlights, with their strong beams, were showing me the way. It was past ten o'clock. I was driving slowly, taking my time. I didn't have any reason to rush.

The six-kilometre road was winding gently between the old, not too tall mountains, densely covered by eucalyptus woods and short shrubs, so characteristic of the Australian vegetation. The winter night sky was clear, and all the constellations of the southern hemisphere were shining frozen on the vault of heavens like an infinity of coloured beads, randomly spread by a gigantic imaginary hand. Outside was shiveringly cold, but inside the car, the air conditioning system was maintaining a pleasant ambient temperature.

I was alone. Not long before, I had left the house where Diane, my dear Diane,, had accompanied me to the door just to say "goodbye". She asked me, with worry in her eyes, to take care of myself. For a short time, I relived the moment of my departure. I was feeling somehow guilty. I was wondering if I was not on the verge of losing my mind. I didn't want any of my loved ones to worry for me. I was leaving the house that night to do an unusual thing… I was aware of that.

That night, I decided to put into practice a decision I had taken not many days before. It was a sudden and surprising decision, but in fact, it was the result of many months of deliberation. While my eyes were following the dark and winding road, my thoughts slowly drifted into the past.

This story began in my childhood. Even at a very early stage of my life, when I could hardly remember, I had witnessed strange happenings. Firmly imprinted in my memory, not even the irreversible flow of time managed to erase them. I didn't understand them, and I didn't pay too much attention to them at the time. Later though, during my teenage years, I began to realise that something was indeed going on, but even then, I blamed it all on my rich imagination.

The years passed, and as their number increased, so did the number of those unforgettable events. No matter how many there were, they remained unexplained. I just didn't know what to believe. Were those memories the product of my own fantasy, or real facts which I was indeed experiencing without my will and independent of my imagination? Questions… questions… and even more questions.

Years later, I read in several publications about the possible existence of a different type of intelligence of unknown origin, considered to be coming from outside our world. I will be honest: driven by immense curiosity, I read that there were numerous cases of ordinary people who were implicated individually and sometimes in groups in this complex phenomenon. They were witnesses of inexplicable events which, when described, sounded incredibly similar to the events I personally experienced over the years.

Despite those similarities, it still felt at least fantastic, if not impossible, that I could be implicated in something like this. Yet, those strange events were a reality, whether I wanted them or not, and they continued to appear in my life and complicate my existence. At that time in Romania, as in most countries of the world, this subject wasn't discussed, much less studied, as it happens today.

I find it hard to explain why, during those years, I never talked about those strange events, not even with the people closest to me. I remember often feeling troubled by some of those weird happenings, which managed to consume me inside significantly and, as a result, I appeared as a changed person to my family and friends. When asked what was bothering me, I just couldn't confess what the real reason was.

I also remember that numerous times, I felt very close to revealing the real source of my restlessness, but I never went ahead and did that. Each time that happened, something in my subconscious stopped me. It was something that felt like a sort of advice with a very convincing power. Thinking back, it was better that way.

Years passed. New unusual events took place in the Danube Delta, that beautiful and untouched part of Romania, so wild and spectacular, which I was so much attracted to and loved with all my heart. I was eighteen years old then, camping together with one of my best friends in a remote area of that wonderful corner of the world, when, despite all our efforts, we just couldn't account for more than eighteen hours of our lives.

A few years later, still in the Danube Delta, during one of the nights, I woke up and found myself in a different place from where I had gone to sleep, feeling unable to move or feel the weight of my body, surrounded by a powerful and penetrating vibration which I didn't understand where it was coming from.

After my 1989 emigration to Australia, more of those unusual events added themselves to the list. Those were the medical experiments that had been performed on me by the same mysterious beings whose faces I couldn't see, or wasn't allowed to see clearly. Without exception, everything was happening during the night. I can't think of a single medical field being left out or not shown as a point of interest. From the nature of our skin, main organs, arm mobility, vision, hearing, resistance to physical stress, all the way to reproduction and sex, everything was studied.

I can firmly confirm that sex was thoroughly studied. The methods used were as exotic as their curiosity. I remember very well a large number of tests that aimed to determine how we think, how we perceive and react to different situations, how we make decisions, including the morality of those decisions. The way we see and understand "right and wrong", and how we react to it.

As far as I could understand, all of that was meant to help them evaluate our level of evolution from a biological and spiritual point of view, and further, the level of advancement we had achieved as humans at this particular time in history. In the last few years, there were a kind of different type of interactions which I decided to call "awareness interactions".

What was different on these occasions was the fact that at the end of every test I was subjected to, I had been marked on the skin in different parts of my body, most of the time on my face and arms, with small burn-type marks symbolising geometric figures. In my opinion, their intention was to let me know that whatever happened on those specific nights was not a dream, but real events they wanted me to remember and start treating as real.

That was the way they tried to make me understand that there was an agenda I should be aware of, and that those were not the products of my imagination or hallucinations. The marks left on my skin were standing proof of that.

As a result of these strange memories, I became a changed person. I stopped being myself. I am a happy, optimistic, and full-of-energy individual. Later, I started worrying when it was time to go to bed. I hated, for no apparent reason, the approach of evening. I was not fearful of people, it was something else I couldn't explain. An internal tension appeared once the evening was approaching, and what was even more frustrating, I couldn't find any reasonable explanation for it.

The memories I had were vague and so unusual that my logic refused to consider them real. By chance, while browsing through a phone book one day, I came across the name of a Sydney organisation that appeared to study exactly this phenomenon. After a long period of hesitation, I finally decided to pick up the phone and make the call.

At the other end of the line, I found someone who was ready to listen to what I had to say. In fact, he offered to meet me the very same day, just a few hours later. Over the following few months, I met other people interested in the same subject. Organised in research groups, they were trying to shed some light on the mystery surrounding this phenomenon.

Very soon, I found out that the only tool which could deliver relative success to this complicated puzzle was hypnotic regression. In the following two years, I had the opportunity to meet three different hypnotherapists. What was revealed through this technique was so unexpected that it overwhelmed my imagination. I had never dreamed it was possible to witness what surfaced from my own suppressed memories.

Unfortunately, instead of finally finding answers to those obsessive questions, many more were rising in my mind. I was running in a vicious circle. One strange event stood out among all. It happened some time ago but, in the aftermath, I realised, or possibly was intentionally led to understand, that those behind the nocturnal encounters were capable of reading, interpreting, and recording my thoughts.

At that time, I felt deeply affected by all these implications. It felt as though I had lost my personality, and I considered what they were doing to be an unforgivable violation of my privacy. Over time, though, I got used to the idea and became indifferent to it. I just didn't care. I had nothing important to hide anyway.

More than that, it came to my attention that, in turn, I could actually check if such a thing as the reading of my mind was true or not. I imagined and later drew on a piece of paper a diagram made of the calligraphic figures imprinted on my skin during the nocturnal events, the ones I called the "awareness interactions". I mentally formulated an invitation to receive a response to this game and, as physical proof of my request, I left the piece of paper on the navigation table in the main cabin of my yacht.

The yacht was moored in a very picturesque place north of Sydney, called Berowra Waters. These waterways are part of the beautiful Hawkesbury River Basin. The river is about 80 miles long and flows slowly through old mountains, passes through Berowra Waters, and finally meets the ocean approximately 26 miles downstream.

I didn't have much hope of getting a response. The attempt seemed childish, even to myself, and yet, despite my expectations, three days later I received an answer. Unbelievable!

The cryptogram I had left on the navigation table, composed of the calligraphic symbols and geometric figures, was asking about the meaning and direction of development of the entire story I had been implicated in. By ingeniously modifying my own cryptogram and using my own logic, someone who knew me better than I could imagine changed my question into an answer:

"–Wait! The story is not finished."

Unbelievable! And yet, the answer was in front of me. Someone up there did care what I was thinking and feeling. A new wave of questions was born. The mystery didn't disappear, quite the opposite, it grew in proportion. The feeling of frustration became almost painful.

In the winter of 1997, I was the subject of some nocturnal events that pushed me to the limit of desperation. I tried everything in my power to find a logical and material explanation for the events I had witnessed during those unusual nights.

I found myself close to finally accepting what, for a long time, Diane had been trying to convince me of, that no matter how hard I tried for an answer, I would never have it. I wondered if Diane was right after all. That was very possible. Yet, I couldn't accept it until I had exhausted every last attempt to find the truth. At that point, I knew I had reached that milestone. It was my last idea, and I was determined not to back off from it.

One of those frustrating days, a thought struck my imagination. The next moment, I had decided, I had to do it. I'll admit it, I was scared. A strange sensation stirred in my stomach just thinking about it, and yet I decided to give it a go. I had to meet those foreign beings in a voluntary and conscious way, face to face.

Now, the next question arose: was such a thing possible? I didn't know for sure, but I was determined to try. Another thought came unexpectedly to my mind. Not long before, I had received that surprising cryptographic response. Logically, it meant that "those someone" were able to read my thoughts. Following that same line of logic, it meant that some form of communication could indeed be possible. It sounded fantastic, but possible. I had nothing to lose.

How was I going to achieve that? Using the power of thought. To my surprise, this trick had worked before. I decided then how I was going to put my plan into practice and where. I chose to use the yacht as the meeting place. I also chose an uninhabited spot on the Hawkesbury River where this unusual meeting could take place.

I decided the date and mentally repeated it for a couple of days, along with the other details, location and time. It might sound like a childish game, but I played it seriously. This time, it was what I wanted, for a change. I prepared myself to accept any outcome, no matter what it was going to be, with only one condition: it had to be the truth. That was the only rule of the game.

Involuntarily, I activated the car's direction indicator and gently veered the vehicle to the right. I had reached my destination. That interrupted the flow of my memories. I slowly left the main road, and a few hundred metres later, I parked my car in front of the marina's building. I stopped the engine, turned off the headlights, pulled the handbrake up and got out of the car. The freezing temperature outside went straight to my bones. The surrounding darkness from the ground made the sky's vault look magical, highlighting its splendour. I zipped up my warm flying jacket all the way and started walking towards the main marina pontoon, where my dinghy was tied up, waiting for me.

Once in the boat, I started rowing at a slow tempo, covering the distance between the pontoon and the yacht. It was silently floating in the dark, a few hundred metres away. While I was handling the oars, I involuntarily lifted my eyes towards the sky above. That impressive view took my breath away. The surrounding dark mountains were arching gracefully from the height of their peaks all the way down to the still surface of the water, as if forming a gigantic parabolic antenna opened towards the limitless universe. Somewhere up there, hidden in the immensity, were those whom I wanted to meet on that splendid night. I was wondering if they were going to come to this meeting. I was also wondering if, in fact, I was at the beginning of losing my mind. Perhaps only Almighty God could give me a true answer. It was too late to back down anyway, and I was convinced that I wouldn't ever forgive myself if I did.

It didn't take long before I reached the yacht. I quickly jumped from the dinghy into the cockpit, unlocked the sliding hatch and entered the main cabin. I turned on the ceiling lights and began preparing to start the diesel engine. I opened the water valves, turned on the main battery switch and pushed the start button. The diesel engine woke up from its deep sleep, coughed and puffed unimpressed several times, but once warmed up, it started spinning quietly, turning off its warning lights and on the ones for control and navigation. I rushed outside on the deck, to the bow of the yacht, and untied the mooring rope. I returned to the cockpit, pushed the gearbox lever into the "forward" position, engaging the propeller to turn freely under the boat. Soon, the yacht started moving slowly, slicing the still surface of the water. Not long after, it reached its cruising speed of four knots.

I was steering the yacht standing up, following with my eyes the pale lights of the lonely houses spread randomly along the shores of the river. They were slowly passing me in the distance and ultimately getting lost in the darkness, out of sight. I knew those waterways very well. Helped by the night navigation lights, I was not worried about losing my way. The chosen meeting place was not that far, around three nautical miles downstream from the mooring place I had just left behind. The freezing temperature made itself stubbornly felt. I was blaming myself for not taking along the automatic pilot, which could have saved me from holding the icy tiller with my bare hands. I was feeling the pain of the biting cold on my fingers while steering the yacht, which was sliding smoothly through the water close to the rocky and unfriendly riverbanks.

After roughly forty minutes spent in the silence of the night, disturbed only by the muffled sound of the engine, I reached my destination. I steered the yacht in a large turn to the starboard side, leaving behind the main body of the river and entering slowly, with the engine idling and the propeller disconnected, a small bay surrounded by steep mountains hidden in the darkness. Once positioned in the middle of the bay, I released the heavy anchor, dropping it into the water until it reached the sandy bottom, securing the yacht in a stable position. I returned to the cockpit, stopped the engine and turned off the navigation lights. I was there. I was where I had planned to be.

Before going inside the cabin, I decided to take one more look at the night's view. It was an unforgettable sight. Dark and mysterious mountains were rising from the water not far from me. The heavens were shining above. The glittering light of the stars couldn't scatter the deep darkness surrounding me down to sea level. The perfectly still surface of the water was covered by the black and overwhelming shadow of the mountains, and because of that, it reflected only partially the splendour of the universe above. The silence was complete, and nature seemed to be frozen by the deep biting cold.

I entered the yacht's main cabin and closed the sliding hatch behind me. I regretted that I couldn't admire as long as I wanted the mysterious beauty of that special night. I quickly looked at the digital clock on the yacht's electric panel and noticed that it was almost midnight. I started rubbing my hands together just to warm them up. On the starboard side of the main cabin, where the little kitchen was, I lit one of the burners of the cooking stove and continued to warm my hands above the blue flame. Soon, a pleasant warm air filled the interior of the cabin. I pushed a few buttons on the electrical panel, preparing the yacht for the night. The little red control lights came on one by one while the ceiling lights went off.

I grabbed a cassette at random from the stack and inserted it into the yacht's stereo system. Finally, I went to bed, covering myself with a thick woollen blanket. I was feeling very tired and fell asleep in no time, more likely before the first melody from the cassette had even finished playing. I had almost forgotten why I was there.

An indefinite period of time passed. Suddenly, I realised that I was dreaming. Strange! … I was dreaming of driving my car on the same winding road I had used a few hours before. It was still dark, and without any warning, the beams of the headlights and the dashboard lights went out. The engine stopped too. I noticed that all electrical power of the vehicle was gone. Didn't take long, and I understood what was happening. I quickly decided to pull the car over, off the road, trying to take advantage of the still-moving vehicle, which was rolling only out of its inertia. I looked outside, and it was pitch black. I was getting scared. I tried to control my fear. I couldn't remain inside the car doing nothing, so I decided to get out and wait right next to it. I had the feeling that I knew what was going to happen.

At this stage of the dream, I opened my eyes. Suddenly, I was awake. I realised that I was still in the main cabin, in the same bed where I went to sleep before. I was lying face up. Very strange! … This is the only position I have never been able to sleep in. My hands were stretched down next to my body in such a way they didn't feel like they were mine. I was completely awake, but the strong feeling of fear still persisted. My entire body was affected by an unusual vibration which I recognised so well. I tried desperately to move but found it impossible to do so. A strange type of pressure, somehow similar to centrifugal force, made all my attempts to move fruitless. It was not painful but very scary. All my commands of movement were inexplicably stopped.

I could hardly breathe and tried to fight the pressure on my chest. I felt pinned down by a force I couldn't see or understand. With great difficulty and a great deal of will, I managed to move my head and eyes slightly from left to right and back again. I noticed that the interior of the cabin was lit by a warm light which I didn't understand where it was coming from. To my surprise, through the starboard windows, I could see multicoloured lights vibrating and blinking with high frequency in total silence, similar to the LED lights of a Christmas tree. I remembered that before I went to bed, I looked through the same windows, and as I expected, there was total darkness.

A new phenomenon caught my attention. I felt a strange sensation behind my palms and forearms. An unusual force was moving my arms. While I was only a frightened witness, both my arms were lifted from their position. They were slowly moved upwards, rotated, and lowered beside my head in a classic surrendering position, ending up on both sides of my pillow. My legs were immobilised the same way, being pushed down by that unknown force. It had such intensity that any attempt to move them was unsuccessful. I was so scared; I can't describe it in words. I am a healthy and strong man, but I found myself stripped of any ability to defend myself. My palms were open, with their fingers stiff and stretched out. I couldn't move them no matter how much effort I made. My breathing was getting heavier, and my fear was growing fast.

Suddenly, I sensed a movement to my left. Surprised and scared, I forced my neck muscles and, with all the effort I had, just managed to turn my head slightly in that direction. My desperate effort was just enough to see from the corner of my eye a small, slim, humanoid-looking creature trying to hide itself from my sight. For a moment, it stayed hidden behind the partition wall between the main cabin and the bathroom, but realising it had been seen, it changed its mind and, in three small steps, came towards me, rushing to grab my left hand.

In that state of intense fear, I couldn't miss noticing in dismay how, driven by a command that wasn't mine, my left hand started moving on its own through the air and reached his hand. That hand was so different from mine, dark grey skin, with very long fingers. I'm not exaggerating when I say they were twice as long as ours. I wouldn't know the number of fingers because they were kept together, close to each other. They were unusually long. I will never forget that.

When our hands touched, a strong and strange feeling took over my entire body. No matter how hard I try, I can't even come close to describing that feeling accurately. The closest word would be: … awe!

The way that creature came into my view, the way it moved towards me, avoiding skillfully the obstacles in its path, and the way my hand moved through the air until it met his and touched, were the most convincing proofs that I was awake and in full possession of my senses. Unbelievable!

For a single moment, that great surprise replaced my fear. I was looking, fascinated, at something I could hardly accept as reality. I was looking at a living being I had never seen before. Its head was larger compared with ours, much larger at the back, with a definitely different shape. Its face was small, almost triangular and expressionless, with a sharp and pointed chin. The cheeks were flat and stern. The skin was dark grey, with no hair anywhere. The eyes were the most interesting feature of its face. They were large, black, slanted, almost touching each other in the middle, giving the face an Asian appearance. The nose was small, almost inexistent, marked only by two small, elongated nostrils positioned above its small, thin mouth. Fantastic!

And yet, the surprises didn't end there. My attention was drawn to something even more unexpected. Right above me, no further than one metre, literally floating just under the cabin's ceiling, was another creature totally different from the first one. How it got there, I couldn't understand. If the first creature surprised me with its look, the second one, no exaggeration, took my breath away. The living being floating above me looked like a prematurely aged child. Because of my position and movement restrictions, I couldn't see for sure how tall it was. I could only guess it was no taller than 1.2 or 1.3 metres in height. Its body was fairly proportioned for its height, with the only difference being that the head was larger than expected. It was dressed in a light-coloured robe with a very simple cut, starting from its neck and ending at its feet. The head was almost round, as you would expect a young child to have it. The skin of its face had an unusually ghostly, whitish-pale colour, totally different from ours. No hair. Round, piercing and very inquisitive eyes, almost hidden by two prominent cheeks, gave the face a Mongolian look. The nose was childlike, small, with two round nostrils above its small, thin mouth, which it kept closed at all times. It looked like a younger version of the mysterious personage I had met in my early childhood, the one whose face I had never forgotten, and which now, more than thirty years later, had come to meet me again, at my own request. Despite recognising that face, and the fact that we were not entirely unknown to each other, it didn't stop me from having such a strong reaction. Those two living beings sitting next to me didn't belong to my world. I was paralysed in amazement. I felt the sensation of an imminent emotional collapse and worried that, because of its intensity, I might never recover from it. I was lying there in the double berth of the main cabin of my yacht, immobilised, facing upwards, with my hands held in that defenceless position. I was staring intensely at something I had never seen in full consciousness in my entire life before. I was in shock, fear and surprise, all three combined. That was not regression hypnosis, and it was not a dream. I knew I was looking at something real, a reality I didn't fully understand. It was the truth I had asked for. My wish had been granted. Now it was my turn to make the effort to accept it. God, how different it was from what I had imagined.

Because of the intensity of my emotions, I felt very close to losing consciousness. At that very moment, a calm, whispered male voice sounded strangely in my mind. I say strangely because the sound didn't come from outside, it came from inside my own brain. The voice appeared to be that of a man, and yet had a note of tenderness in it. It was repeated twice. It gently told me:

"Don't be afraid… don't be afraid…"

I can't explain why, but I just knew that the being floating above me, one metre away, was responsible for this message. One more strange thing took place, our eyes met. Suddenly, we were looking into each other's eyes. That was an experience that can't be fully described in words. I felt that I had lost my identity. I felt like an open book in which that unknown stranger had the ability to read absolutely everything he wanted. Incredible! The process seemed to be working both ways. Fantastic!

Only by looking into each other's eyes, we were communicating. Surprised, I realised that I was receiving answers to questions I hadn't even had the chance to mentally formulate yet. It seemed this stranger could not only read my thoughts but also guess my intentions. Unbelievable!

I looked intensely into those deep black eyes, and my mind was working feverishly. With amazing speed, I was flooded with wave after wave of information. I worried that I would not be able to memorise it all. I wanted to take time to retain everything, but the information came so fast that I was forced to abandon that idea. It seemed all the information was being channelled and stored in my memory automatically, with no effort on my part.

I was told that this meeting was different from the ones before. I would not be part of any type of testing on this occasion. I was also told that I would be allowed to remember this meeting as long as I could control my fear and avoid panic. The fact that I had voluntarily decided to meet them openly marked an important and unexpected step in the relationship between us. I was told that I had been immobilised in that defenceless position as a precaution, to prevent me from hurting myself or them in the event of sudden and uncontrollable fear. I was told that the dream I had during the night had been artificially induced, with the intention of reducing, as much as possible, the psychological shock I was going to be exposed to upon awakening to that challenging reality. He also explained that, for the same reason, during the meeting, both of them would keep my biological parameters and level of psychological stress under constant control. By reducing the level of perception of the sensory nervous system and employing other methods, such as various sound and light signals to the brain, they were able to control the amount of stress so that it would not overwhelm my psychological tolerance. Instantly, I realised that what he was telling me was logical, and it was the truth.

Because of his explanation, I suddenly understood why, during this unusual nocturnal meeting, since those two strange beings appeared in my cabin, my ability to perceive and my entire thinking process had been continuously interrupted every 10 to 12 seconds. In that painless and inexplicable process, my brain appeared to short out, much like flicking a switch "off" and "on" again. Almost instantly, the brain would fully recover its functions for another 10 to 12 seconds, after which the whole process repeated. I realised that those two nocturnal visitors knew much more about us than I could imagine. By interfering with my thinking process and reducing my level of perception during moments of elevated emotional stress, they managed to keep me relatively calm and observant. Physically, I was restrained and therefore couldn't move, yet I was physiologically aware, interactive, and stable. They achieved all that by using the two most basic human instincts: fear and curiosity. They did it in a very intelligent way. Interrupting, for short and repeated periods, the functions of the brain brings about in us an involuntary and unconditional need to regain those vital functions as quickly as possible, while simultaneously creating a strong sense of curiosity, the need to find out what happened, what caused that interruption, and what the immediate surrounding situation is. Once this process starts and is continuously sustained in this clever way, the permanently maintained curiosity almost completely removes the other basic human instinct: fear and self-preservation. Unbelievable! … and yet so logical!

Fear and the conservation instinct were, and continue to be, instincts that throughout our evolution helped us survive as individuals and as a species. They helped generate foresight and stimulated our creativity. Unfortunately, when fear reaches elevated levels, it becomes destructive, transforming into panic and hysteria, often causing far more damage than the initial source of danger. Curiosity, on the other hand, is what transformed us from creatures of the animal realm into technological beings. It governed our progress. Undoubtedly, throughout our evolution, these two instincts were inseparable and omnipresent. What made human beings what we are today was curiosity, which has always had a far stronger effect on the individual, most of the time overcoming the instinct for self-preservation.

I was lying in my bed, immobilised, facing the ceiling, pushed down by a strong unknown force that made my entire body vibrate from every single cell. I was looking directly into the eyes of that strange being who was so different from me. In those moments, I completely lost all feeling. I was witnessing such a surprising experience that my emotions no longer mattered. I instantly understood why those two living beings, the messengers of a civilisation so different from ours, who had arrived from who knows what corner of the universe, had chosen exactly this ultimate human quality as their means of approaching me: curiosity. Our need to discover what we cannot yet understand. That was, and will always be, the force that helps us overcome the unknown and, above all, our own fears. Those three simple words, telepathically whispered in my mind, gently underlined their intentions. They had physically come to meet me, at my own request, to remind me of this prime condition necessary for commencing our communion:

"Don't be afraid... don't be afraid..."

Suddenly, the pressure keeping my entire body immobilised began to ease, and before long, it had entirely disappeared. I was surprised by this unexpected and sudden change and tried to find an answer from the two strangers beside me. I looked around and found nothing. They had vanished as mysteriously as they had appeared. I felt so overwhelmed that I had to make a huge effort to calm myself down. I was still lying on my back in the main cabin's double berth. My muscles finally began to relax, as after a strenuous physical effort. That internal vibration faded, and I could breathe much more easily. I began to feel generally relaxed. I brought my arms back from that strange position but found them numb and weak. I tried to stand up in the bed but found it difficult. I was still deeply affected by what had happened and was desperately trying to remember as many details as I could of that extraordinary experience. The interior of the cabin was again in darkness. The small blue round flame of the stove, still burning, couldn't pierce the shadows around me. I rubbed my forehead slowly with my hands, more to convince myself it wasn't a dream. A thought came to my mind, and I decided to act on it. I quickly opened the access hatch and jumped into the cockpit. I raised my eyes to the sky and began searching for something I expected to see up there in the heavens.

Unbelievable! Just above my head, a very strong source of light was climbing into the sky at great speed, on a perfectly vertical trajectory. I looked upward in fascination as that bright light disappeared into interstellar space. I followed it with my eyes in amazement for more than thirty seconds. Its size became so small that I almost lost sight of it when it suddenly changed its trajectory, approximately 30 degrees to the south, and continued climbing into infinity. Soon, it completely disappeared into the immensity of the universe from where it came.

Farewell, strangers! I slowly sat down in the cockpit, resting my right arm on the yacht's tiller. I moved my fingers gently up and down its smoothly curved shape. What direction would I take now? What would the future hold for me from this moment on? I had just received one of the greatest gifts I had ever wished for. My heart was pounding strongly in my chest from the emotions. At that moment, I felt grateful for my destiny, for the chance I had been given to live such an experience. I was lucky, and I decided I would remind myself of it forever. My thoughts carried me away for a while until I realised I was shivering. Regretfully, that I couldn't admire the silent beauty of that night for longer, I left the cockpit and returned to the warmth of the cabin, closing the sliding entrance hatch behind me. Out of habit, I looked at the digital clock on the yacht's electric panel, it was four o'clock in the morning. I soon fell asleep and woke three hours later as the sun began to climb slowly into the sky. It was a charming morning. Nature was fully enjoying the beginning of a new day in its paradise. I pulled up the anchor and took the yacht back to its mooring. I rowed my little dinghy to shore and, once there, started walking towards the parking lot where I had left my car the night before. I started the engine, lowered the side window, and let the car roll slowly along the road. The same radio station that had played romantic music the night before was now broadcasting the latest world news. The fresh, invigorating morning air, with its eucalyptus scent, flooded my lungs, making me feel optimistic and full of energy. I was impatient to reach home and tell Diane what had happened during the night. I could hardly wait to start writing the story of this extraordinary Australian winter's night.

The End.

Chapter 2:
The Ultimate Dream

True Story

Part 1: The Missing Time

Many years ago, I made a promise to someone, a promise, until now, I haven't kept. It is a long story, and you will understand later why I kept it to myself. I have never forgotten it, and all these years I kept thinking about it.

Through the nature of my work, I spend a lot of time travelling all over this big Australian continent, which gives me the opportunity to look back at my life and memories.

Long flights and long hours spent behind the steering wheel, most of the time in the middle of the desert, are the perfect ingredients for my mind to slide back in time.

One day, while driving, I was listening to the radio and, by chance, came across a story that sparked my curiosity and opened the gate of my memories. Intrigued, as soon as I had some time to spare, I searched the internet for stories with similar content. I was surprised to find that several other people were telling stories that described the same thing I thought only I knew. Over the years, I had spoken very little about it, and only to a few people close to me. Those who lived such extraordinary events gave different interpretations, but no matter how they perceived them, I understood exactly what they were trying to say. What they described, I had lived myself. There was no mistaking it. Regardless of their intelligence, language, culture, or religion, it made no difference, they were all describing the same thing, and it had the same overwhelming effect on them as it had, and still has, on me to this day and forever.

If curious, here is the story:

The summer of 1978.

Black Sea Coast, Romania, Europe.

I was an 18-year-old teenager and, like all teenagers, full of energy, dreams, and restlessness. That summer school holiday was a little different from the others. At that time, I was a member of a high school singing group, and we sacrificed half of our free time preparing for an autumn concert tour in Italy. Unfortunately, because of this commitment, I couldn't join my friends on our yearly Danube Delta expedition. I felt quite unhappy about that, but a promise is a promise, and I didn't want to let anyone down. I enjoyed being part of that choir and always loved music. I loved water sports far more than anything else, and missing the Danube Delta expedition was hard to accept. For the last eight years, every summer that was the event we dreamed of, organised, and trained for.

The choir rehearsals were going well, and I was trying hard to hang in there, but in the end, I said to myself, "bugger that," and told our conductor I would take a week off rehearsals and go to the Danube Delta for a change. He wasn't happy, but I didn't care. He went nuts when he found out I was taking Justin, my best friend, with me too. Justin was part of the same group and was very keen to escape into nature together. We grew up together, lived close to each other, and had been classmates since primary school, the best buddies to this day.

We planned to spend a week somewhere in the Danube Delta, camping on a bank of a water channel between a small town named Maliuc and a large freshwater lake called Fortuna. We knew the area well from previous expeditions, and we chose that location because we didn't need a boat to get there, it was close to the town for supplies, and, not least, the beauty of the place.

Just the two of us and our basic camping equipment travelled by train at first, then by passenger ship to the small town of Maliuc. Once off the ship, we carried our equipment on our backs through the dusty streets of the town and probably a couple more kilometres outside it. We followed the bank of the channel, looking for the best spot to set up our camp. We picked a nice spot across the water and used our inflatable camping mattresses to float the luggage over. We protected our things by swimming on each side of that improvised raft, and with a little luck, managed to move all our belongings across without getting them wet. It was fun and a little adventurous, exactly what we wanted.

The camp was set up in no time. We had done this so many times that it was now routine. We also learned to keep track of the time when the mosquitoes started to become active. There was a period in the evening, between seven and nine pm, when it was almost impossible to stay outside without being severely bitten by those little annoying insects. No insect repellent or protection method really worked. After nine o'clock, we could finally enjoy the peace and tranquillity of nature. That was the time for cooking, eating dinner outside the tent, night fishing, or listening to music on our little battery-operated transistor radio.

The daily routine was simple. We got up in the morning, and the first thing we did was make the fire. A simple breakfast, followed by one or two cups of peppermint tea, tasty and refreshing, made from the leaves of the peppermint plants growing all around us along the channel banks. We spent most of the day swimming and fishing, then prepared the fire again for the evening. When the mosquitoes went away, it was time to cook the catch of the day and enjoy dinner next to the campfire. The night sky was spectacular in that part of the world, and most of the time we contemplated it in silence until we'd had enough and went inside the tent to sleep. Not bad… not bad at all.

A couple of funny events remain in my memory from that short trip. One night, we were both awakened by the sound of heavy footsteps coming from somewhere around our tent. It was an uneasy sound that made us nervous. Our tent was set in a wooded, isolated area, at least two kilometres from the town's last houses. We didn't have any other camping neighbours, and in the middle of the night, anyone walking around couldn't be a good sign.

After an unnerving period of listening and worrying about it, I decided to go outside the tent to confront the uninvited guest. I grabbed our small axe, which we kept inside the tent during the night, and stepped out. That small axe was used for cutting firewood and was essential when hammering the steel pegs into the ground to anchor the tent.

I opened the tent's fabric door as fast as I could, jumped outside in a commando roll style, got on my feet, and with the axe in my hand, I was ready to strike anything which could pose a danger to our safety. Well, that anything happened to be a stupid cow. With her front legs spread apart, her head down and her confused face staring at me, she looked at least as scared as I was. We both didn't move a hair for about 30 seconds until we realised who was what, and then just turned our backs to each other. She went away into the darkness, and I went back inside the tent to sleep, relieved that it was only a false alarm.

Thank God the axe didn't get to be used that night, but it almost got me killed the following day. Sometime around lunch, we decided to go and collect some dry wood for the upcoming evening campfire. There were plenty of trees around and no shortage at all of wood to burn. Walking among the trees, one of us got the "brilliant" idea to throw the axe into one of the tree trunks, just to see if we would be skilful enough to get it stuck there, like the native North American Indians used to do with their tomahawks in the movies when fighting the White People.

Didn't take long and this stupid game became a serious competition. Well, like any stupid idea, it didn't last too long; someone was going to get hurt, and that someone was going to be me. It happened to be one of my turns to throw and when the axe hit the tree trunk I aimed for, it didn't get stuck there but bounced back and fell on the ground nearby.

I rushed quickly to pick it up and try again, but when I got close to the axe, a strange buzzing sound could be heard nearby. By the time I realised what the sound was, it was already too late. A strong stinging pain went through my back and hundreds of bugs were flying angrily, circling me. It happened that my axe hit a wild wasp's nest and as a result of that, their defence instinct got triggered and I got bitten in the back by at least one. The pain was strong, and the panic that followed was even stronger. A small number of those bites was known to kill a horse. I didn't want to end up in that situation and the only idea that came to my mind to save my arse was to run as fast as I possibly could to the water, jump in it and stay under for a while until the angry wasps were going to give up on me. It took some time, staying under the surface and just raising my head high enough to breathe. The wasps finally let me live with a warning. Those bites hurt me like hell, but I was alive and that was a little miracle in itself.

Young, restless and looking for trouble. We just kept going. We made the fire, waited for the mosquitoes to go away, and got ready for cooking. I took the bunch of fish we had caught during the day and got them to the water channel, with the good intention to give them a quick wash. Still in pain and fairly miserable, I was trying to do the washing without getting wet; but wasn't to be. That happens when you are trying to be too careful. I lost my balance, my legs went into the air, and my whole body went into the muddy shallow water. I was a mess. Mud everywhere; on my clothes and on my face. Justin, who witnessed the whole scene, couldn't help himself and instead of keeping his mouth shut, made one of his annoying smart remarks:

"Oh, I forgot to tell you, that area where you were might be slippery," he said, and the prick ran away laughing. The schmuck ran away just in time because the entire bunch of fish was flying through the air towards his head, followed by my curses. Son of a gun. Happy, happy times. Only us trying to have fun.

Sometime during that week, towards the end of our stay, something weird happened. One morning, just after breakfast, we noticed that our food supplies were going down and there was a need to go back to town for some basic shopping. As I was still in pain because of the wasp bites, Justin offered himself to do the trip. He left soon after finishing drinking our peppermint tea, taking with him an empty backpack to carry the shopping. The distance between our camp and the town was around two, two and a half kilometres, and taking into consideration the time for crossing the water channel, it shouldn't take him more than one hour, one hour and a half to return. He did come back but came back empty-handed. He had a strange look on his face but whatever the look was, gave me the impression of confusion. I asked Justin why he didn't bring any food back from the shops and his answer was simple and surprising. The shops were all closed. He arrived in town after 5 pm in the afternoon. He was puzzled and so was I. How the heck was that possible? We had just woken up half an hour before he left and with the time added for his travel, he should be back and still have a couple of hours before lunch by our calculations. We couldn't be sleeping through the entire day and yet here we were, late afternoon, with the shops closed and us with no food. Theoretically, eighteen hours of continuous deep sleep. That was nuts. We were in the middle of August and in this period of the year, the daylight starts very early, and the mornings tend to be fairly cold due to the morning dew. Because of that low temperature, we used to wake up early in the morning and for the same reason we loved to drink our favourite hot peppermint tea at that time of the day, to warm ourselves up. Justin and I felt bloody confused for a while and told that story to everyone on our return from that camping trip. We laughed a lot about it, but we have never really been able to explain how it was possible for two young, fit and healthy teenagers to lose almost an entire day simultaneously sleeping. It just didn't make sense and yet that was what happened.

The world kept spinning, and many years passed since then.

Part 2: The Book

Fifteen years later.

1993. Sydney, Australia.

One day, I happened to be with my daughter in a library. We were looking for a children's book she needed for school. She had the freedom to choose anything she liked, and I let her take her time picking whatever appealed to her young and curious mind. To fill my own time there, I began browsing the shelves for something to read.

In the Nonfiction section of that library, there was a book that caught my attention. On its cover was printed a face that mesmerised me. A strange-looking face, I felt I recognised it, though I wouldn't know why or from where. I picked the book up from the shelf and kept looking at that face. It wasn't the unusual features that affected me most, but rather the pair of large, black, slanted, almond-shaped eyes that almost hypnotised me.

I was holding in my hands the book *Communion*, written by Whitley Strieber. The impulse to find out what was hidden behind those black eyes was so strong that I left the library borrowing the book and took it home with me.

Whitley Strieber, an American writer, told an unusual story in that book, the story of his life and his involvement in something he hadn't expected and didn't fully understand until much later. I will not judge the subject or the story of that book. His interpretation of the events he described, I consider sincere and powerful. It is not a story you would read every day, and it is certainly not a story for everyone.

Speaking for myself, I will admit that his unconventional book began a long process of wondering and frustration. As a writer, he was free to tell any story he considered worth telling, and he did just that. What I found extraordinarily frustrating was that some of the stories or events included in his book sounded very similar to stories and events I could recall from my own life. That was the most frustrating thing.

There were times when I just had to stop reading, put the book down, and boil in my own soup for a while. Was I losing my mind, or did I simply happen to have similar memories of the same kind of strange events? I have long since learned that it is very important to be, above all, honest with yourself... and there was the dilemma. Was I, in my subconscious, trying to deceive myself by associating some of Strieber's stories with mine? Or was there another possibility, that we had both actually lived similar experiences? What was the truth?

Part 3: Going Back in Time

It is said, "time heals everything." Well, it didn't happen in my case. That book triggered something in my mind which didn't go away. I was growing more and more frustrated with every week that passed and wanted to put an end to it. Easier said than done. My life was already fairly complicated at that stage, and my frustration didn't help to make it any better. One day, I came across an ad in the Sydney Yellow Pages. It was an advertisement from a research group interested in finding people with stories like Whitley Strieber's and potentially stories like mine. After many days of hesitation, I finally made the phone call. The person who answered the phone listened to what I had to say, and in the end, he offered to meet me for a more detailed conversation. It was too late to back out, and I accepted his offer. A few days later, we met. I invited him onto my boat and we sat together talking in the main cabin over a cup of coffee.

At that time, I was living half of the week on my yacht and spending the other half with my English girlfriend, Diane, in her apartment somewhere in Sydney. As I was saying before, my life wasn't that simple then. My new acquaintance and I had a long chat about Strieber's book, and he listened carefully to what I had to say about my strange feeling that I might have had similar experiences too. I mentioned to him only a few of my vague and intriguing memories, similar to those described in Strieber's book. At the end, he said there was only one way to really find out what had happened in those instances, to have at least one session of regression hypnosis. He explained to me briefly what the process of regression involved and emphasised that, due to the nature of those long-past events and their likely intense emotional content, the mind tends to block such memories for self-protection and preservation.

I felt that Don, that was his name, could be right, and his advice might be the beginning of the end of my frustration. I agreed to meet the person who was going to perform the regression hypnosis on me. A few days later, he introduced me to that gentleman, and we met at his office somewhere in Sydney. His name was Robert; he was a professional hypnotherapist and part of the same research group to which Don also belonged. I liked Robert from the very beginning. He was a man in his late fifties, well-spoken and extremely well-read, considering the hundreds of books on the shelves of his office. He already knew why I was there from his colleague Don, and after a short chat, he explained to me what regression hypnosis was all about.

It turns out that our brain possesses two different types of memory. The first type is the active one we use day by day, minute by minute. This type of memory is part of who we are and works together with our consciousness, recording everyday events and storing them in such a way that we can access them when needed. This memory is called short-term memory; it filters what is important and forgets what is not. There is a second type of memory that records everything from the day we are born to the day we die and is stored in a different part of the brain, in such a way that we cannot access it consciously. It is part of our unconscious mind. The only way of reaching this passive type of memory and bringing it to the conscious mind is by putting the brain into a form of trance through relaxation.

Regression hypnosis has been used for many decades and is considered one of the best tools for investigating a person's past events that, under normal conditions, have long been forgotten. What is amazing is that regression hypnosis brings back to life all sensations and emotions identical to those experienced by that individual in that particular place and time, no matter how long ago it happened. To put it simply, under regression hypnosis, you will see what you saw, hear what you heard, feel what you felt, and witness what you witnessed, no matter how long ago it occurred. It is amazing that this is possible, but I will admit, having never done it before, I had no idea such a thing could be real. The human mind is a miracle, and it remains a mystery to us.

Don, Robert and I met three times. In the first two sessions, despite all the techniques and effort Robert put in, nothing happened. I was unable to relax my mind and body to the level needed for the remembering process to take place. I felt disappointed and almost ready to give up. Robert, however, was confident that he would find a way to reach what we all wanted. During our third session, Robert asked me which particular event I wanted to remember. Without hesitation, I told him that I wanted to know what actually happened to us on the night we ended up sleeping continuously for eighteen hours. That had happened fifteen years earlier, during that camping trip in the Danube Delta, in 1978.

Robert was a man who didn't give up easily, and for the third time he began the process of relaxation. The way he did it proved to be very interesting. I was told to concentrate on my breathing and, with every breath, to let go of all my physical and emotional tension. With each breath I took, the tension seemed to disappear, starting from the muscles of my head, neck, shoulders, and arms, all the way down to the muscles of my toes. In that state, I truly felt a total physical and emotional relaxation. It was an amazing feeling, one we should all try to experience whenever life pushes us to our limits. No wonder so many religions promote the same state of calm through prayer or meditation.

Once there, Robert asked me to imagine that I was in an elevator. The elevator would close its doors and begin going down through a shaft of time. He told me to imagine that every floor the elevator passed represented one year in time, and asked me to press the button on the control panel showing the year 1978. The power of imagination!

I followed Robert's advice and did what he asked me to do. I placed myself in that elevator, travelling down through time. I could see the years passing by, and when the elevator gently stopped, the year displayed was 1978. The doors slowly opened, and the dim light inside disappeared. I was back in the pitch-black darkness of my tent, on that August night, on the bank of the channel in the Danube Delta, in the year 1978.

Part 4: The Ultimate Dream

I didn't know what time it was, but I could sense that something wasn't right. Outside the tent, there was a humming sound, and I could feel a strange vibration in the air. That humming was similar to the noise produced by a powerful transformer, and the vibration felt pretty much like being in front of a very large speaker that was generating some extremely low-key sound waves which I could feel penetrating my body but not hearing them. I opened my eyes and tried to make sense of what was happening. For a few moments, I just lay there on my back, wondering what that could be. With every second that passed, the vibration was becoming stronger and stronger. Soon, my entire body was also vibrating with the same low frequency. I was worried that because of that very high intensity, I was going to ultimately disintegrate; it was that powerful. My instinct was telling me to get out of the tent and escape that situation. When I tried to get up, my body didn't listen to me. I tried and tried again. My mind was sending the commands to the muscles with no response from their part. A state of great panic flooded my soul. For a short moment, I thought of death. I thought that I had died and what was happening was part of that process. I was convinced it was the end. I was so frightened that I find it hard to accurately describe it in words.

At the peak of that nightmare, something else just started to happen. My body was lifted from the ground and slowly started ascending vertically in a straight line. The sensation of being lifted was a totally new one. In a normal condition, I should feel the inertia of my body. I was expecting to feel the different movement of my arms, legs, head, and so on. The lifting I was witnessing was incredible. Every single cell of my body was moved instantly in absolute synchronicity. The kinetic inertia was missing; just pure, slow, upward ascension which somehow gave me the feeling that it was intentionally controlled. To the unbearable state of fear I was already in, was added the feeling that the balance of my body during that movement wasn't perfect. I was being lifted in a horizontal position, and I could feel slight corrections were applied to maintain it so. My eyes were open and in the darkness of the night, I was just able to see that by now, I was already well above the treetops of the wooded area where we were camped. The fear of being dropped from that height to the ground was just added to my nightmare. The vertical movement stopped after an indefinite period of time, and I could feel instead that I was sliding quite fast on a horizontal trajectory. As before, there were slight corrections applied to the balance of my body just to maintain its horizontal position. I was not able to approximate how high I was, but I did feel the low temperature of the atmosphere associated with high elevation. There was nothing to reduce my fear and most probably, I passed out.

When I came around and opened my eyes, it took me a few good seconds to realise where I was. A dark and humid environment, with the air thick and difficult to breathe. Some kind of fog was present in the air, and wherever I was, I couldn't see anything familiar. I also couldn't move. What I was hoping to be a simple nightmare proved to be reality. The fear and sentiment of panic returned painfully. I found myself lying on my back on some surface, which I was not able to see but only feel. My arms were in a classical surrendering position. My legs were slightly apart, my arms were kept firmly pushed against that hard surface, with the forearms high above the shoulders and the palms almost touching my neck, as if I was summoned to surrender. My fingers were stretched out and stiff. I felt very scared, helpless, and vulnerable. There was a pressure all over my body that pinned me down. I had never experienced such a thing before. I was restrained by something I didn't understand. It was applied from the top, on my legs, chest and abdomen, arms and head. It was a static pressure I couldn't beat. The only thing I could still do was move my eyes and very little my head. I felt like a trapped animal waiting for its fate.

To add even more horror to my state of mind, I just noticed three or four silhouettes coming in my direction. The very little source of light seemed to come from the periphery of what I could only assume to be a room. Having such a dim light coming from behind them, I couldn't distinguish their look until they came very close to me. Seeing their appearance was the ultimate shock. I wasn't only scared; I was petrified. Those silhouettes weren't human; they didn't look like me. Disproportionately large heads with relatively small triangular faces, thin lips, small mouth, no noses but only two nostrils above it. The most impressive feature of their faces were the eyes, large, black, almond-shaped and slanted. I was scared out of my mind. They came closer to where I was lying, and one by one came and looked at me face to face. I had the impression that they wanted to introduce themselves in silence. Their expressionless faces looked severe and showed that they were different individuals. In turns, each one came and looked directly into my eyes for a few moments. Every time I felt that they could read me like an open book. Just by looking into my eyes what I knew, they knew. Scary; it was very, very scary. I felt completely under their power, and I hated that.

I decided not to give up that easily but to fight. I tried to use my physical strength to get out of that situation. I tried several times to stand up. Each time the pressure on top of my chest increased to levels almost intolerable and as a result, my efforts were unsuccessful. I could hardly breathe and thought I was very close to losing consciousness.

"– We would prefer if you remained in that position, please…" I heard a voice telepathically addressing me.

Whaaauuuu… that was new!

At that time, I could speak Romanian, basic French, English, and German. They talked to me in none of those languages. They didn't even use sound to communicate with me. They just put that message into my mind without using words, but just the meaning of them. Very, very strange and effective. I definitely understood their polite but also firm demand.

"– You are kept in this position for your own protection.– We will not harm you. We will perform a physiological examination, and you will be returned to the place where we took you from," the voice explained.

Moments later, the restraining pressure on my body increased again to a level almost intolerable. The examination was just about to begin. I couldn't see those silhouettes anymore. A strange greenish light was shown in front of my face. Later on, I understood that the light was designed to calm me down and varied in intensity according to the level of stress I was in. Without any warning, my left arm started moving on its own. That was a very weird feeling. That was not my action. It was totally out of my will and control. From that surrendering position where it had been kept, my arm slowly moved to a new position, down towards what I could only assume was the floor. A strong pain came from the thumb of this arm and soon the entire palm felt very cold. I didn't know what was happening with my arm, and struggling to breathe, I just managed to complain about it. A few moments later, a numbing sensation replaced the pain. I was grateful for that, and I thanked them for listening and doing something about it.

The following fifteen to twenty minutes were as extraordinary and surprising as the entire experience. Trying to summarise it the best I can, whatever they did was an experiment focused on my arms, their mobility in all possible positions, and the endurance of the arm muscles. It was interesting to find that they were particularly interested in the arms positioned behind my back. We all know that in this position our arms are the weakest in terms of mobility and strength. Why was I not surprised? They had total control over their movement, and they abused that power many times. I complained each time their curiosity caused me pain. I will be honest and admit that each time they realised the experiment was causing pain, they asked permission to go ahead or not, and they also stopped when my pain became too much to bear.

Those twenty minutes of experimentation were a non-stop dialogue between us, and they always backed off when my complaints became too loud. It was so extraordinary. Those beings, who didn't look like us, knew us so well. Because in most of the critical moments they hid themselves from my view, and because they maintained continuous conversation with me, my level of fear almost disappeared. I was so relieved that I didn't feel in immediate danger anymore, and I made a point of thanking them for allowing that to happen. Yet the most amazing part of this experience was just about to begin.

The experimentation focused on my arms appeared to be coming to an end, and feeling relieved and grateful, I thanked them again for taking my complaints into consideration. I was so happy that it was over. At that time, my right arm had been fully tested and was now resting alongside my body, with my palms on top of each other on my abdomen. It was not going to stop there. Moments later, the right arm started moving again. It was the same unknown force that miraculously controlled it without my will or any input. It gently rose from its resting place, slowly moved upward, turned its palm backward, and with the back of my fingers, touched gently upon my forehead. I was pleasantly surprised by this beautiful, tender, and unexpected gesture.

The telepathic voice came back into my mind:

"– Do you like that?" I was asked.

"– Yes, I do… thank you," I answered.

Well, from my forehead, the fingers started moving very slowly, just touching my eyebrows, down the side of my right eye, moving gently over my cheek, slowly across my nose and lips, down to my chin, and up again on the other side of my face. The way the fingers slowly and gently touched my face was unbelievably tender and beautiful. I was speechless. The only thing I could do was say, "– Thank you," again.

"– Did you like that?" the voice asked me.

"– Yes, I did… I did indeed, thank you."

"– Why did you do that for?" I asked.

Instead of answering my question, one more unexpected thing happened. My right arm started moving again and slowly changed its position from my face, resting gently on the right side of my chest. It was another tender gesture, and my intuition was that they wanted my palm to rest on top of my heart. I couldn't help myself and said:

"– The heart is on the other side of the chest," I said.

"– I believe you wanted to rest my arm on top of my heart. The heart is on the left side of my chest. You probably got confused," I added, being cheeky.

"– Why did you do that for?" I repeated the question.

It seemed there was indeed a small mistake on their part, because soon, they slowly moved my arm and gently rested it on top of my heart, in the correct position this time.

"– Because we love you," they answered.

I knew instinctively that they were referring to our entire world and not only to me as one entity. I was in awe.

"– Are you going to forward this message to your people? … Can you promise us that?" the voice continued.

"– Yes, I promise," was my answer.

"– I promise," I chose to say again.

It appeared that they were happy with my response. As a result, in a very unexpected way, I was shown the image of a light. Its source was somewhere deep in my view and from the centre it glowed, emanating the most pure and overwhelming feeling of love. A light I had never seen or witnessed before. It was the most pure and warm light I could ever imagine. It emanated balance, truth, trust, honesty, happiness, and ultimate love. Seeing that light, I now know what all those people in the internet documentaries were trying to describe.

Some call that light "The Love of God." Some, "The Secret of the Universe." And some call it simply "The Light." This is what so many others were talking about. They were as affected by it as I was, and seeing it for themselves made that experience worth living. I don't know if my story will do any justice to those beings I encountered forty years ago. I am happy instead that I finally have the opportunity to keep the promise I made to them such a long time ago.

I was asked to say that we are not alone, and we all have a common destiny, no matter our position on the ladder of evolution. The goal to be achieved is reaching eternal harmony and love. We are all one, and one all.

Us, Them, and the Others, aspiring for the ultimate dream… to reach "The Light."

The End.

Chapter 3:
Floating Away

A Holiday Romance

Danube Delta

Romania, Europe

The youngest and forever-changing Romanian territory, the place where the mighty Danube River meets the Black Sea. A land where life is mostly untouched by modern civilisation, and where the flora and fauna are colourful and exuberant, in a harmony which only Mother Nature is capable of displaying. Hundreds of interconnected freshwater lakes are spread between three large river branches, fed by the old Danube at the end of its journey, stretching from the Black Forest in Germany, throughout Europe, all the way to the Black Sea.

Most of our childhood, during our school summer vacations, my brother Peter and I used to go and explore this vast and beautiful part of the world. Members of a nautical club, we could hardly wait for summer to come, and every year, for at least two weeks, we enjoyed the wilderness of that land and water. Gathered in four or five crews of two, in our wooden kayaks, accompanied by two more transport boats, we paddled our way all over this large area, and through the years, our love for it only grew.

Peter and I are different people. Most siblings born one after the other are like that. There are a lot of things we could never share together, but the love for the Danube Delta is not one of those. Even to this day, each time we talk about it, our memories are equally filled with the same love, passion, and nostalgia.

I will admit it, for me there is one more reason the Danube Delta is so special.

If curious, here is the story:

The year 1979. I was nineteen years old. That year was a good year. In June, I attended, passed, and enrolled as a student in the Faculty of Mechanical Engineering, part of the Polytechnic Institute of Bucharest. Finally, there were no more high school classes, uniforms, and, most importantly, no more studying for a while. I was facing three full months of summer holiday, followed by one year in the Armed Forces (the National Service), followed by three more months of holiday, and only then, five years of university. It didn't sound that bad at all.

My brother Peter, who was only one year older than me, had just been released from his military service, and now he was looking forward to the next stage in his life as a university student. We both were going to leave our family home and start a new life on our own, my brother moving to the country's capital, Bucharest, to study, and I to my military unit for one year, and only after that to join him in civilian life.

The first two weeks of that much-wished-for holiday we spent in Constanța, our hometown. During the day, we were on the beautiful beaches under the summer sun of the Black Sea, and in the evenings, you could find us at the seaside restaurants and bars, drinking beer and socialising with our friends. Even such a great lifestyle can become a little too much when it repeats over and over again. At that point, we knew there was a need for a change. We agreed that the best idea was to spend some time visiting our magic place, the Danube Delta. We decided to go there for a couple of weeks, first just the two of us, and later to be joined by some of our friends.

It didn't take much preparation, and soon we were on the train to Tulcea, the gateway city to the Danube Delta. At its river port, we bribed a ship captain and got two seats in a fast passenger boat that was transporting a new lot of student tourists to a camp named the "Red Lake Tourist Centre." That was our intended destination. We knew that place very well from our previous expeditions, and the beauty of it was that it perfectly combined the glamour of nature with the vibrant and exciting lifestyle of young people, most of them our own age.

A few hours later, we were there. Once arrived, we met with some of our local friends who were in charge of the administration of the centre, and after we paid for food and accommodation, we became part of the six-day tour.

The touristic centre was located in the middle of a two-kilometre-long channel, who was connecting two very large freshwater lakes, all together, only a very small part of the multitude of lakes and channels that made up the Danube Delta. The centre itself was arranged in two halves: on one side of the channel were the accommodation cabins and sports fields, and on the other side, a large restaurant and a clubhouse in two different buildings.

To facilitate the crossing of the approximately 30-metre-wide channel, each cabin was allocated a fibreglass rowing boat. This idea was just brilliant, it solved the problem of crossing the channel from the cabins to the restaurant and bar and back, and at the same time gave tourists the opportunity to discover for themselves, during their stay, the beauty of their surroundings.

Those waterways were breathtaking, crystal-clear waters, a multitude of beautifully coloured water plants, the bright green of the reeds, and the invigorating activity of hundreds of species of fish and water birds the Danube Delta is well known for. That was Water Paradise.

In the late hours of the afternoon, we were already outside on the bank of the channel, with a couple of drinks in our hands, enjoying those beautiful surroundings and watching the activity of the newcomers. The weather was great. The approaching evening came with no wind, clear skies, and a warm temperature. In the campsite, most of the newly arrived visitors had finished settling in their cabins and were now getting ready to cross the water for dinner.

The students came from all over the country, and for some of them, handling a boat was not something they had ever done before. We really couldn't blame them for that, but still, it was interesting to watch. Some of them were jumping into their boats, which were still half resting on the sandbank, and then waiting for a miraculous force to push them out into the deep.

Some were sitting on the rowing seats facing forwards, like in a car, trying to use the oars that way, and finally, some just got it right from the beginning and managed to cross the water safely. One by one, the fleet of rowing boats reached the other side, except for one.

Two girls were walking around their boat, just looking at it. They didn't seem to know what to do, and just sitting around wasn't going to solve their problem. Somehow, I felt sorry for them. I entered the water and swam across. I asked if they needed my help. Their answer was as expected, they did. The boat was too heavy for them to push into the water from the sandbank, and even if they could, they didn't know how to row it anyway. I offered to row them across the channel, and the girls accepted with undisguised gratitude. Once we arrived on the other side, my brother helped me secure the boat and also helped the girls out. We introduced ourselves, and the girls did the same.

We started walking together towards the restaurant and, to our surprise, we were invited to share a table with them for dinner. We ended up spending the rest of the evening in their company. Celine and Simone were their names. They had been good friends for many years, and they had both just graduated from medical school that summer when they decided to go, for the last time together, to this camp in the Danube Delta, a place neither had visited before. That was to be their final adventure together before starting their careers as doctors.

Our story, obviously, was not that long, but we offered to show them around if they were interested, promising that they would not be disappointed. Simone and Celine accepted with enthusiasm. The deal was good for both parties: we would get access to a boat, and the girls would get to see the Danube Delta in all its splendour.

After dinner, we said goodbye to each other, not before rowing them back to their cabin. That was the first of six unforgettable days we spent together that summer.

As promised, the next morning, after breakfast, all four of us left the camp using their boat. Downstream along the channel, a couple of kilometres away, there was a place few people knew existed, and it was the perfect spot to experience the beauty of the Danube Delta. Peter managed to borrow an extra pair of oars from our local friends at the camp, giving us the opportunity to row the boat in tandem, twice as fast.

As I mentioned before, we spent most of our childhood around boats, and in our high school years, other than swimming, we both trained in academic rowing as a performance sport, participating in many national competitions. Rowing was one of those things we were really good at. I don't mean to sound boastful, but looking back, I believe that after so many years of physical exercise and training, being young, tall, well-built, suntanned, and rowing the boat shirtless at a slow tempo, Peter and I didn't look bad at all in the eyes of Celine and Simone that day. But let's get back to the story.

Not long after leaving the tourist centre, we found what we were looking for. There was a very narrow, well-hidden entrance to a shallow channel. It was so shallow that Peter and I jumped out of the boat, leaving the girls inside, and physically dragged the boat through. A few hundred metres later, our efforts paid off. The narrow channel revealed a well-hidden paradise. We had entered a lake no larger than two or three square kilometres. The water was crystal clear, revealing abundant aquatic vegetation from top to bottom. Red and green towering water plants tried to hide large groups of multicoloured small fish, chasing each other around. On the surface, beautiful white and yellow water lilies were opening their petals on vivid green, round leaves. The rippless water was disturbed only by the lazy paddling of wild ducks, pelicans, and swans enjoying that peaceful summer day. Noisy and playful seagulls glided through the air, adding even more life to that amazingly beautiful scene. I find it hard to describe in words the beauty, wilderness, and purity of that place.

We let the boat drift in silence towards the middle of the lake, fearing that talking might spoil its magic.

Celine and Simone were quiet, fascinated by the beauty, and only later, on our way back to the camp, did the girls admit that what they had seen was far more beautiful than they had imagined.

After lunch, the temperature rose a little, and we decided to go for a swim. It was the perfect way to cool down. We jumped into the boat again and rowed upstream along the channel until we reached a large lake that Peter and I knew was the best spot to swim. There was no wind, so the water was calm. The water was clear, and its temperature was just right. After rowing a few hundred metres further towards the middle of the lake, we stopped. With no reason to stay in the hot sun, Peter and I jumped in.

Simone and Celine needed a little more encouragement. They told us neither was a strong swimmer, but the call of the cool water was hard to resist. The girls removed their clothes, wearing only their swimming costumes, and slowly lowered themselves into the water from the aft of the boat. I watched them from a distance as they entered the water. They both looked very attractive in their costumes. I was pleased to see Simone start swimming in my direction, probably to feel more comfortable being next to someone more confident in the water.

We spent a long time swimming, chatting, and giggling around our slowly drifting boat. At one point, Simone confessed that she felt protected being close to me in the water. I won't deny, I liked hearing her say that. It boosted my confidence. The truth was, I had felt attracted to her from the moment I first met her, the way she looked, smiled, and spoke. She never made me feel the age difference; Simone was seven years older than me. As a teenager, I had been fairly shy around girls. I was the quiet type. Occasionally I felt close to some schoolmates, but nothing ever went beyond small flings. Peter, on the other hand, had always been ahead of me in that regard. I didn't mind; he was the "big brother" after all.

When our swim ended, I climbed back into the boat and helped Simone out of the water. For a girl, that wasn't easy. Gently, I pulled her out and held her in my arms for a few moments longer than I probably should have. I just couldn't help myself, I wanted to feel her skin against mine. It felt good, and even better when she smiled at me just for doing that. Her smile was reward enough to put her down.

The evening was drawing in, and we left the lake, rowing back to the camp just to get ready for dinner. Not long after, we met up again. We waited for them to cross the channel together on our way to the restaurant. The girls looked wonderful that evening. I really hadn't expected to see them so nicely dressed, and I could hardly hide my surprise. Simone was wearing a short, light-coloured dress that fitted her slim figure well and complemented the tone of her skin and hair. I couldn't take my eyes off her during dinner, and I had the feeling she didn't mind that either.

The night was fresh, and after dinner, we invited them to the club for drinks. The club was the place to be. It was packed with most, if not all, of the students on the tour. Beer flowed freely, the music was great, and the atmosphere buzzed with youth and happiness.

I asked Simone to dance with me, and we ended up spending most of the night on the dance floor. Some of the slow songs gave me the chance to hold her in my arms again. I loved the feeling of her body against mine. I liked the way she moved and the way she accepted me as her only dance partner. She was a feminine and attractive woman.

Late that night, when the club closed, we accompanied Simone and Celine back to their cabin.

Just after I said, "Good night," I kissed Simone on the lips. In the dim light at the cabin entrance, Simone looked into my eyes for a moment, smiled, and kissed me back.

Her kiss was not just a "good night" kiss. It felt different. It was the kiss of a woman to a man, long, warm, and passionate. I held her gaze for a few moments… and smiled.

I wished her "good night" and left. That was the end of a very special night. I didn't want to spoil it.

The next day, after breakfast, it was planned for all four of us to spend the morning on the water again. We wanted to show the girls a second large lake nearby, famous for its large colonies of pelicans and swans. Those magnificent birds were in great numbers there, enjoying the abundance of fish, their primary food source. I don't remember the exact reason, but Peter and Celine decided not to come along. I had the feeling they had been invited by some local friends, perhaps for pike fishing or something similar. I asked Simone if she still wanted to go ahead with our original plan, just the two of us. She agreed, and we left the camp shortly after finishing breakfast.

The morning was more than pleasant. The air was comfortably warm, with a light breeze coming from the sea, carrying a salty aroma that, combined with the scent of sun lotion on our skin, reminded us we were still on holiday.

I started rowing at a slow pace. There was no need to rush; the day had just begun. Fifteen or twenty minutes later, our boat emerged from the channel and slowly entered the large lake we planned to explore. I continued to row towards the middle. We had no other plans for the day. The shores of the lake were barely visible through the morning mist. From a distance, we could already see what we had come for: large groups of pelicans socialising undisturbed. Here and there, we saw fishermen's nets, and from time to time, small fish leapt from the water, frantically trying to escape their predators. Nature was showing us its beauty.

While I rowed lazily, Simone talked, and I only half paid attention. I liked listening to her voice, and for me, that was enough. She told me stories from her years at medical school, what I could expect to experience soon, and offered some advice she thought might be useful.

"-Looks like I'm the only one talking today, Victor," she said, probably testing my attention.

"-Maybe because I'm a little nervous, I guess," she continued.

"-Only us, alone in the middle of nowhere," she added.

I looked at Simone in surprise. I initially wanted to reassure her there was nothing to worry about. I didn't want her to feel uncomfortable. Instead, I stopped rowing, leaned gently towards her, and kissed her. As slowly as I did, I leaned back and started rowing again. Simone looked surprised at first, but soon she smiled. She came close and kissed me back.

It happened there, in the middle of the lake, on that slowly drifting boat, in the gentle sea breeze and under the cloudless summer sky. Simone offered herself to me in a gentle and very sensual way. She was a woman, and I loved the way she made me understand that. It is said we never forget our first time. I couldn't have asked for a better memory.

After midday, I started rowing back to the camp. Something felt different, and it felt bloody good. Suddenly, I felt more confident. I believe a new spark had appeared in my eyes, one that remains with me to this day.

We arrived back at the camp just in time for lunch. We met Peter and Celine, and everything returned to normal. We spent the rest of the day in much the same way: sunbathing, swimming, chatting, laughing; dinner in the evening, dancing at night. Two more days passed in the same rhythm. But there was something different now… Simone and I were not just good friends; we were lovers. And that was how the last night of the tour found us.

After dinner, we went to the club, as we had every night. As midnight approached, the atmosphere grew heavier. Few words were spoken, just the music and our thoughts. We never talked about the approaching day. It felt as if time had frozen and the last day would never come. Yet, here we were, at the inevitable end.

I was young, but not naive. I realised our lives were heading in two different directions. Deep down, I knew our destinies were not meant to stay on the same path forever.

Almost at midnight, I asked Simone to leave the club and come outside with me. Once there, I told her I wanted to show her something special if she wanted to see it. Simone trusted me and agreed. For the last time, just the two of us were in the boat, rowing in the dark. I kept the boat in the middle of the channel, drifting downstream towards the same lake where we had made love for the first time. We entered it, and as before, I rowed towards the middle. Half an hour later, I stopped rowing and let the boat drift.

It was a glorious night. There was no wind, and the lake's surface was frighteningly still. There was no sound, no movement at all. The sky above was crystal clear. Billions of stars and galaxies shone like a gigantic chandelier, covering the sky and reflecting in the mirror-like water. It was magical. The image was so overwhelming it felt as if we were in the middle of the universe. Unforgettable, indescribable. The sense of infinite space made us feel like two people floating in eternity. That was what I wanted to show Simone. It was my way of saying, "I will never forget you and our time together." I knew she would remember that moment as I do, to this day and forever.

The following morning, Simone and Celine boarded the fast passenger ship and returned to their previous lives. Peter and I did the same six days later.

The Danube Delta remained as beautiful as ever, but for me, it was no longer the same. Something felt missing, and sadly, I knew it would never come back.

In autumn, I joined my army unit, **"The 1st Tank Regiment – Tudor Vladimirescu"**, in the middle of the country, and spent almost a year in the armed forces. It was a basic officer school for those intending to become engineers. I loved it. It proved to be exactly what I needed. I loved the impressive and powerful T55 Russian-designed tank we trained on, the night and day driving and shooting exercises, the long and tiring marches, and the camaraderie we built between our platoon soldiers, a camaraderie that lasts to this day. I respected the army uniform and its traditions. We were lucky our service took place in peacetime, when nobody shot at us and we didn't have to shoot back. We joined the Armed Forces as boys and returned as men. What a great experience.

The following summer, it was my turn to recover from the social isolation the army, as an institution, tends to induce in a former soldier's behaviour. It took a little while to fully feel like a civilian again, but eventually, I did.

The first year of university was also a good year. Almost at its very start, I joined **"Song"**, a student singing group much loved across the country. With it came a new wave of fun and unforgettable memories. It wasn't necessarily a love for music that drew me in, but rather the pretty girls in the group. Despite all the activities and shows we had that year, it was a miracle I managed to pass all seven of my exams and tests in the summer session. Because of that, I found myself free to enjoy the following three months of carefree fun. To my parents' disappointment, during those three months, I was everywhere but home. Student camp on the Black Sea Coast, a trip to the Danube Delta, a mountain student camp, singing tours, everywhere but home.

In early September, I finally ran out of places to go and things to do, so I decided to return to Constanța, my hometown, and spend some time with my family. Only a few days remained of the school holiday, and it seemed only fair to remember my parents, who had so generously financed all the fun I'd had in the previous three months.

Autumn on the Black Sea Coast is a nostalgic season. I've always had that impression. The usually packed beaches were now empty, the hotels and restaurants had only a few guests, and the mornings and nights grew colder, just reminding us that winter was on its way. In those nostalgic conditions, we tended to spend more time at home, especially in the evenings, when we shared family dinners.

One quiet evening, during dinner, my mother was telling us about her day at work. She worked in a very large municipal hospital in our city and, as a medical technician, belonged to the Blood Testing Laboratory. I've never liked hospitals. They are places of suffering most of the time. People don't go there for fun, it's definitely not a happy place. For that reason, stories about hospitals and what happens inside them never interested me much, so that evening, I was only half paying attention to my mother's story.

She was telling us that during the day, she came across a young female doctor who needed to have her own blood tested. The young doctor worked in the same hospital but in a different department. My mother tried to help her as quickly as she could, offering to process the samples and provide the results as soon as they were ready. The young doctor agreed to wait while the samples were processed. That was how the two women began talking. No surprise there, especially knowing my mother's curiosity and love for chatting.

During their conversation, my mother discovered the young doctor was in her second year of practice and was just about to get married. That was one reason for the blood tests, she wanted to ensure she and her future husband were ready to start a family. My mother, God love her, kept asking questions, and naturally, the conversation turned to children. The young doctor, like most women, enjoyed talking and answered all my mother's questions. Inevitably, they ended up discussing having children. My mother, in her curiosity, asked if the young doctor intended to have children. That's when it became interesting. The young doctor smiled knowingly and confessed:

"– Oh yes," she said.

"– Of course, we want children… at least two," she added.

"– I'll tell you a secret," she smiled again.

"– Two years ago, a friend and I met two boys at a student camp in the Danube Delta during our holidays. Those two boys were brothers, a few years younger than us. Hard to explain how, but they stole our hearts and made us feel very special for a while. Now that I think about it, I would love to have two little boys, and when they grow up, to be like those two brothers we met on that holiday two years ago. Their names were Peter and Victor."

My mother's face dropped in surprise, and at the dinner table… so did mine!

"– I have two boys, students in Bucharest, who go to the Danube Delta every year together, and their names are Victor and Peter, believe it or not," my mother replied instantly.

Now it was the young doctor's turn to look surprised.

"– Are you the mother of Victor and Peter?" she asked, astonished by the coincidence.

"– Yes, I am," my mother answered. "– They are my boys."

The table went silent for a moment. I didn't expect to hear that, especially after so much time and in such a way. I immediately started asking questions. I asked my mother if she had taken her friend's phone number and if she knew where the young doctor's office was in the hospital. My mother already had all the answers.

The next morning, following her directions, I was at the hospital, knocking at the office door. A few moments later, Celine opened it and, with her sincere and happy smile, invited me in.

The only reason I left that office that morning was that people outside were waiting to be consulted, and they were certainly in more need of medical assistance than I was. I was there for a bleeding heart, nothing more.

I met Celine that day again. She invited me to her house in the afternoon, and we spent a lot more time together. She told me that on the day we said goodbye, two years before, and for a long period afterwards, Simone had been really affected and quiet. She had wanted to find me but couldn't, as we knew nothing about each other at the time. Eventually, she gave up. Celine also said that she and Simone were no longer in contact, and all she knew was that Simone had taken a post in Bucharest. The only thing she still had was an old phone number.

Two years seemed to vanish in an instant. I felt the same way I had on the day she left. Late that night, I dialled that phone number. Simone's voice came back to me from the other end:

"– Hello?"

"– Hi Simone… it's Victor… how are you?"

"– Victor? … Oh God! … I'm okay… how are you?"

"– I'm okay too… it's been a long time, Simone…"

"– Long time indeed, Victor… long time indeed… where are you? … Where are you calling from?"

"– I'm home in Constanța… I just met Celine by chance today… believe it or not… after so much time, I met her… that's how I have this number… where are you?"

"– I'm in Bucharest, Victor… I work here now."

"– I want to see you, Simone… is it possible?"

"– I want to see you too, Victor… but it must be the three of us… if you don't mind. I'm married now… I'll meet you with my husband if that's okay… what do you say?"

"– I just want to see you, Simone… of course it's okay… I'll meet you both."

The next morning, I travelled the 250 km to Bucharest by train. That evening, I met Simone at her house.

She opened the door for me, and there she was, the same Simone I had met in the Danube Delta two years before. She was wearing the same short, light-coloured dress that fitted her slim figure perfectly and complemented the tone of her skin and hair. The same dress she had worn the night we first danced together. I smiled, unable to hide my surprise. She smiled too, in complicity. By now, she knew I remembered. That was our secret to keep that night.

I was invited to stay for dinner, and I couldn't refuse. I met, of course, her husband, a military surgeon himself, and we spent a long time talking about that trip and many other things we found in common.

I left Simone and her husband late that night and took the train back home to Constanța.

Alone in the train compartment, I gazed through the half-open window into the darkness, listening to the monotonous sound of steel wheels rolling over the rails. I was reflecting on what had happened over the past forty-eight hours. I felt good; I felt at peace.

Seeing Simone again and seeing her happy was all I had wanted. She belonged to another man, and I was okay with that. I needed closure, and I had found it. No regrets, just great memories. The memories of those six days and six nights would stay with us forever. The magical Danube Delta had made it all happen.

Someone once said:

"– The best things in life are the people you love, the places you've seen, and the memories you've made along the way."

I believe it's true.

The End.

Chapter 4:
A Trip Out of This World

"...the highest point a man can attain is not Knowledge, or Virtue, or Goodness, or Victory, but something even greater, more heroic and more despairing: Sacred Awe!"

—*Nikos Kazantzakis, Zorba the Greek*

True Story

Part 1: The Night on the Old Saint George River

It may seem hard to believe the story you are about to read, and I wouldn't blame anyone for that. Thirty-six years ago, I happened to travel somewhere far away... outside our known world. Where exactly? Hard to say. At the time, I didn't even dream such a trip was possible, and yet there I was, witnessing the limitless splendour of the universe... I was in awe.

Have I imagined it? No! I may have an imagination, but I could not imagine the unimaginable, I am not that imaginative.

Here is the story:

July 1986

Black Sea Coast—Romania, Europe

I was 26 years old, a young engineer, just out of university. Once my studies were complete, I thought it was time to start following my dreams. One of them was to design and build my own sailing boat. Living on the Black Sea Coast, I had grown up around boats of all types, but my favourites were sailing boats. Not many people in the country owned one, especially sailing boats. Only a few companies built them in Romania, and most of their products were for public use rather than private ownership. I had always dreamed of owning one and nothing would stop me from making that dream a reality, not the cold winter, not the lack of materials or proper tools, not even the sarcasm of family and friends. I was not easily discouraged.

I started building it at the end of autumn, after graduation, and worked on it through the winter whenever the weather allowed. By the beginning of summer, my boat was ready for its first sailing trip. It was four and a half metres long, with a round hull, and its design was inspired by the Finn Olympic-class sailing boats. I had modified the rigging, adding a jib in front of the mast to the bow, and also included rowing oars so I could navigate shallow and narrow channels where sailing was impractical.

I finished building it just in time for summer. With the warm weather settled, I had the chance to test it and gauge its performance. I found my new boat fulfilled all my expectations and was ready for the long-planned two-week trip in the Danube Delta, away from home. As planned, I was not going alone. My girlfriend, Helen, would be sailing with me. We had met at university four years before and had been almost inseparable ever since. We had lived the carefree student lifestyle: skiing in the winter in the beautiful Carpathian Mountains, boating in the summer in the Danube Delta, and trying to pass our university exams in between, just so we could afford the activities we loved.

That year, the plan was to sail together from the launch site at the 2,000-year-old ruins of the ancient Greek city of Histria, cross the largest freshwater lake in the country, located at the southern border of the Danube Delta, navigate a number of interconnected channels to our favourite place, the Red Lake Tourist Centre, meet my best friend Justin and his girlfriend, spend a few days in that aquatic paradise, and return the same way to Histria. A total of 160 km over fourteen days, in one of the most beautiful places on Earth.

Well, without my knowing, the journey would take me far beyond that.

The first day of the long-awaited trip started well. It was a near-perfect summer's day, with a mild sea breeze gently pushing our sails across the large freshwater lake, Razelm. Late in the afternoon, we were almost at the other end, but not quite. Unfortunately, the weather was about to change, and not for the better. Towering cumulonimbus clouds were gathering, signalling an approaching summer storm.

Lake Razelm is notoriously shallow, rarely more than two metres deep, and with strong winds, such summer storms can generate high, breaking waves. My small boat would not cope well. I didn't want to risk capsizing and sinking it, so I decided to find a sheltered spot on the eastern shore to ride out the storm.

As darkness approached, I observed that the coastline wasn't suitable for landing, its sandbanks were too shallow. The only option left was to remain at anchor nearby. After quickly eating, Helen and I tried to get some rest. Easier said than done. My boat had never been designed for sleeping, and after much rearranging of our luggage, we managed to carve out enough room to lie down.

Our next problem was the mosquitoes, who, excited by the approaching storm, were twice as aggressive as usual. We hurried to cover ourselves as best we could. Finally, just as we were getting comfortable, the storm began. Luckily, the centre of the storm wasn't directly over us, but the strong winds, blinding lightning, and deafening thunder were impressive. We were spared the heavy rain, experiencing only a light shower. Tired from the day's excitement, we somehow managed to fall asleep.

Very early in the morning, when the sun wasn't even up on the horizon, the cold and the wet blankets we were covered with brought us back to reality. The boat we fell asleep in wasn't floating anymore. It was resting on a sandy beach, slightly leaning to one side, with the anchor and the anchor's rope missing. It was very probable that, through the stormy night, the continuous movement of the boat driven by the wind and waves, had rubbed the anchor's rope until it gave way and let our boat, we were deeply sleeping in, run ashore. Considering what we went through that night, that outcome wasn't that bad though. We happened to be actually extremely lucky. We ended up on a sandy beach, not too far from the place we had been anchored; there were no rocks the hull could get damaged by, and the boat itself was intact. Helen and I were cold but, despite that, we did get some sleep and, more importantly, none of us were injured. The sun rose over the horizon slowly in the sky, the temperature became pleasant, and soon the entire cold night was forgotten. Just before pushing my boat back into deep water,

I had the idea of trying to look for the lost rope and anchor. As the water in that area wasn't deep at all, after only a few minutes of searching, I found them both. Now, I was really satisfied. That was the only anchor I had with me, and to lose that on the very first day of the trip was going to be a problem. An anchor is always a very safe and handy thing to have on board, even for such a small boat like mine.

One hour later, after we had breakfast and hot coffee, with our spirits up again, the sails were pushed by a gentle morning breeze, and the boat was happy to take us to the northern side of the lake, where we were going to find and enter a channel a couple of kilometres long, which had at the other end a very well-known tourist location named Portiţa. The resort we were looking for was situated on a very thin and long piece of land positioned between the Black Sea and Lake Razelm, the lake we had just crossed a day before.

That channel had a hidden entrance, which was hard to visually find, and it took me some time until I could be confident that I had positively identified it. I was happy that by now Lake Razelm was left behind and the beautiful Danube Delta lay ahead of us. With the wind pushing our sails from behind, the boat was sliding nicely through the water towards the channel's entrance.

Without any warning, our swinging keel hit something, and the hull started scraping on some invisible underwater rocks. That terrible sound went straight through my heart. We had just hit an underwater rock wall hidden under the surface. My brand-new boat went straight through that wall and ended in the middle of the channel, where the water was deeper. Miraculously, she was still floating. Initially, I thought that was the end of it, and all my work and hopes were ruined. Soon, after I quickly checked the bilge, I noticed that we were not taking on water, and the hull had coped well with the impact. That was the good news. The bad news was that our rudder had broken its hinges and now it was inoperable. I was heartbroken. I just knew that without our rudder, the trip was over, and we somehow had to go back home. At that very moment, one thing was clear: we couldn't stay where we were, and I decided to reach the tourist centre of Portiţa for help. Luckily, I could still use the oars for propulsion, and half an hour later we were arriving at Portiţa's main pontoon. I just couldn't accept my defeat, not on the second day of the trip, and not for the trip I had dreamed, worked, and planned the entire year. I left Helen, who was still shaken by the damaged boat, and started looking for help. Luck happened to be on my side. At Portiţa, there was a construction site at that time, and by asking around, I found a construction worker who was also a welder. Together, we rebuilt the broken hinges out of some mild steel, drilled and welded them together, and installed them in position on the transom of the boat and also on the detachable rudder. It was a rough job, but it was going to do for a while, and it did, as was proven later. I considered myself lucky to find that decent, simple man, ready to help me. I paid him for his effort and thanked The Old Man from Above for my luck. Our improvisation worked well, and a couple of hours later, our boat was ready to sail again.

The second day of the trip proved to be as full of bad luck as the first one. I couldn't understand what the hell was going on; and then it struck me. All that bad luck we had experienced appeared to me to be because my boat hadn't been christened. In the mad rush to finish building it, in the mad rush to get all the preparations done in time for the departure day, we forgot the most important thing: to christen her. Helen and I decided not to take any chances anymore, and on the same evening at our camping place, we performed the traditional ritual of vessel christening, to the best of our abilities. As we didn't have in our provisions a proper bottle of Champagne, the closest we could get was to use some of our precious vodka instead, which we had plenty of. Mariner's tradition says that a woman should perform that ritual, and as Helen was going to share her nickname with the boat, she got the honour to do it. She filled a full glass of vodka and splashed it all over the bow of the boat, chanting while she was doing it: "I name you Bibi, and I wish you always favourable winds and gentle seas." Well, I must admit that from that day on, we haven't had another episode of bad luck. The Universe just wanted to remind us that such mariner's traditions are worth keeping and convinced us to respect them. A little later, I had done it, and finally we were at peace, knowing that what could be done from our part had been done.

Next morning, we were at the wonderful gates of the Danube Delta, that magic place so dear to my heart. From Portiţa, we entered one of the most beautiful channels I have ever seen. The Dunavat Channel stretched over more than 25 kilometres and was the classic example of how amazing nature can be. No wider than 15 to 20 metres, the channel was flanked on both sides by a multitude of swamp trees, which leaned their branches over the water, creating a living tunnel in which our boat cruised. Using the sails was out of the question, of course, and we found ourselves lucky that we didn't have to lower the mast just to go past the living ceiling of leaves. The strong smell of the swamp, the light breeze blowing from the sea, and the nice shade we were under made that journey a living dream. Rowing in the middle of it and following the curves of the channel made that day go slow and peaceful.

In the evening, as planned, we reached the end of that beautiful waterway and set camp on the bank of the third large branch of the Danube River, which, together with the other two, was flowing slowly towards the Black Sea. Saint George Branch was one of my favourite places to sail to. It was a wide, slow-moving mass of water that had always reminded me of the Old Mississippi River from Mark Twain's books I read in my childhood.

The following day, we sailed our boat almost to its end, where the Saint George Branch met the salty waters of the Black Sea. That day was an easy one: no rowing, just the quiet sliding through the water, pushed from behind by a favourable wind. That was my paradise. Just before reaching a small town with the same name as the body of water it was built next to, we entered a narrow channel, a little different from the one we encountered on the third day of our trip. The Ivancea Channel was going to take us to our final destination: the Red Lake Tourist Centre. There, we were going to meet my best friend Justin and his girlfriend. He was going to come from the opposite direction, making his way in a rental rowing boat. We were planning to spend a few days together in that beautiful place. The Red Lake Tourist Centre was the best place to meet. We knew there were good camping opportunities, many amazing places to visit, great fishing spots, night entertainment, the lot. What a lifestyle.

It was one small thing that didn't fit that well into this picture, and I was trying to ignore it as much as I could. I really don't remember exactly how it happened, but I believe it all started with a mosquito bite that got infected. Positioned on the upper left leg, just under the swimming costume line, it didn't have a chance to dry out and heal. Rowing and sitting in that area, combined with perspiration, didn't help, and unfortunately, we didn't have any proper medication to successfully treat it. It was uncomfortable, but I could deal with that. It didn't stop me from enjoying my time in my favourite place, with my favourite people.

Justin and his girlfriend arrived on the day they were expected and at the place we had agreed to meet. We set camp next to each other and spent four unforgettable days together. The daily routine was pretty much the same: fishing, swimming, sunbathing during the day, and dancing at night. How much better could it get?

I will never forget one of those days when we decided to sail to the sea. We left our camp early in the morning and returned just before sunset. What a great day!

From the campsite, we sailed our boat across the Red Lake, probably ten to twelve kilometres, and at its end we entered a small channel, which took us to one of the uninhabited beaches of the Black Sea. We ended up on a beautiful and deserted beach, where we dragged our boat onto its sandbank and spent many hours in that amazing environment, sunbathing and swimming, just to cool down when the temperature became a little too high. Chatting and laughing, and swimming again in the sea. The sound of the waves breaking on the sandy shore, the nice cool breeze, the playful games of the flying seagulls, and the strong smell of the seaweed made that place feel tranquil and wilder than we could have wished for.

Late in the afternoon, we pushed our boat back into the channel, got the sails up, and navigated our way back to the campsite. On the return trip, we were all tired and quiet. The only sounds we could hear were the gentle whistling of the wind, the sound of the waves, and the sensual Latin American music coming from one of the radio stations played by our little battery-operated radio-transistor. A great way to finish a great day. One of those days I wished would never end.

But it did, and not much later, the time came for Justin and Christine to leave us. They had to row back to the village where their boat was hired from, and we had to make our way back to the pick-up point, the ancient ruins of Histria, at the other end of Lake Razelm. We had three to four days of travelling ahead of us. We were again on our own, just me and Helen, for the return trip. I didn't mind that at all, of course, but there was the same little thing I was not looking forward to: the rowing. The infected mosquito bite hadn't healed, and despite the care I took to keep it dry and sterile, the area had become swollen and painful. It was uncomfortable and hurt, especially when I was rowing.

Unfortunately, I was facing at least two days of continuous rowing, which, of course, worried me a little.

The first day of the return trip was, as I expected, a difficult one. Rowing for a good few hours with no interruption proved uncomfortable, but we managed to reach the Saint George Branch, where we set camp on one of its shores. The next day, a stroke of luck hit us, and the wind increased in strength, blowing from a very favourable direction. As the Saint George Branch was wide enough, I took full advantage of that and used the sails most of the day. By evening, we were very close to my desired destination, the entrance to the Dunavat Channel.

As the mosquito bite's time was approaching, we decided to quickly set up camp, have dinner, and try to get a good night's sleep. My leg was hurting me, and I wanted to rest it as much as I could for the following day, which was going to be a full-time rowing one.

With the boat tied to a tree, the tent upright next to it, and a light dinner, we fell asleep in no time. It is hard to say what time it was. From my dreamless, deep sleep, suddenly my mind became aware of a very strong feeling of fear. I wanted to stand up to see what was going on, but I couldn't. I wanted to change my position and couldn't move a thing. My entire body was vibrating in a strange way. I could feel that vibration penetrating my body from head to toe. My eyes were closed, but through my eyelids, a strong light was coming through. Even being blocked that way, the light was blinding and painful.

My arms were laid on my chest next to each other, with the palms and fingers stretched out and stiff. I tried desperately to move them from that position and found it impossible. That vibration was very strong and felt like my entire body was being bombarded with radiation passing right through me. The scariest thing of all was that I didn't feel the weight of my body. I felt as if I were floating and couldn't decide where I was. Other than the strong light shining through my closed eyes and the strong vibration, I could hear a very low, muffled sound in my ears. It sounded like I was next to an extremely powerful electrical transformer.

It is hard to describe the terror I was in. I thought of death, a very painful and scary death. I had major problems breathing because of the fear. It was awful. I was scared out of my mind. The helpless feeling added to the painful fear, and I almost lost consciousness when I had the sensation of slowly regaining the feeling of my weight. I felt myself being lowered and somehow laid down on the ground. A few moments later, the strong vibration that had paralysed me began losing intensity. A few more moments later, it entirely disappeared. The light from above stopped, and slowly I could catch my breath. I started feeling my fingers and soon regained control of their movement. The only thing that didn't go as easily was the fear.

Still breathing heavily, I thought about what had just happened and had no idea what it was. All I knew was that it felt unbelievably terrifying. I will not exaggerate when I say it took me more than 15 minutes before I dared to move my body again. The first thing I did was check on Helen. In the darkness of the tent, I couldn't see a thing, but I gently reached out and touched her to make sure she was there. She was sleeping peacefully, as if nothing had ever happened. A strong feeling of relief took over me. I was there in the tent, and Helen was right next to me. I was back in all my functions, and everything that had just happened felt like a terrifying nightmare… or… was it?

Suddenly, I felt physically and mentally exhausted. I hated the idea of going back to sleep, but I could hardly hold my thoughts, and I decided to close my eyes. I just didn't want to experience that terrible fear again. I fell asleep thinking about it.

When I woke in the morning, the sooner I opened my eyes, the entire episode came back to mind. I sat for many minutes in my sleeping bag, trying not to disturb Helen, and kept thinking about the terror I had been through during the night. It was the first time in my life I could remember such a terrifying event. I wanted to think it was a bad dream, but no matter how hard I tried, the vivid memory of what happened dragged me back to reality.

Daylight and the rising sun, along with the sounds of nature in the early morning, gave me the strength to leave the tent, go outside, and start preparations for our departure. I was not looking forward to that part of the trip. We were going to leave the Old Saint George Branch and enter the beautiful Dunavat Channel again, rowing more than 25 kilometres to the entrance of Lake Razelm. That meant I would be in pain and discomfort most of the time due to my unhealed mosquito bite.

The night before, I was really worried, considering that it seemed to be going from bad to worse every day. Thinking about my leg infection and worrying about it, I suddenly noticed that at that very moment I didn't feel the pain or discomfort I was expecting. I gently touched the affected area with my fingers and found that it was not painful at all; the swelling was gone, and at the same time the pain too. I could feel my leg as normal as the other one, maybe a little numb where the infection had been. That was a great turn of events. I didn't understand how such a thing could happen, but I was definitely happy with the outcome.

Suddenly, I felt much better, and my spirits were high again as if nothing had ever happened. The intense and fearful night memories were replaced by relief and confidence that I would fully enjoy the remaining time in my favourite place in the world.

When Helen woke up and came out of the tent, I was myself again, happy and full of energy. I was more than ready to enjoy the rest of the trip back home. I didn't mention anything to her about what happened that night. For some strange reason, every time I wanted to mention that event, my mind backed away from the idea. Hard to explain. Maybe the best way to put it is that deep inside, my mind was telling me that the story was best not to be told, but left alone. For some unknown reason, I listened to that advice and did just that. Helen never knew what happened on that unforgettable night in the Danube Delta while we were camping on the bank of the Old Saint George Branch in that summer of 1986.

We returned safely to our hometown, Constanta, got married later that year, and had our daughter born in September 1987.

Three years later, all three of us left Romania and settled in Sydney, Australia, where we still live and work today.

Life is an unpredictable and complicated thing. Our roads took us on different paths, and we separated two years later. This happens to many couples for far too many reasons. Well, it happened to us too. We still have two things in common nobody will ever be able to take away from us: the love for our daughter and the unforgettable memories of those beautiful years we spent together.

Part 2: Among the Stars…

1994. Sydney, Australia.

Someone said: "every day is a good day." Every year should be a good year too. Well… some better than others. An intense year on all fronts would be the perfect description for 1994.

I was trying my best to "keep smiling," as the British people say. Believe me, it was not that easy. New job, new relationship, new home. One single thing remained the same: the strange, periodical night events. Just after the separation between me and Helen, I rented a granny flat on top of the hills, in a mountain area in suburban Sydney called Berowra. Several months later, when the landlord decided to put it on the market to be sold, I decided that renting a house for one person wasn't for me anymore. I moved my few things into storage, and myself onto the yacht. Not a bad lifestyle for a young and single man. It was not what I wanted, but I had to keep going forwards; there was no other foreseeable alternative for me at the time.

I had just finished a short contract as a mechanical designer and, desperate for a source of income, I applied for a mechanical technician position at the marina where I used to be a client. My new workplace was only a few hundred metres from where my yacht was moored, I had everything I needed for day-to-day life, and I was free… most of the nights. A lot of weird stuff happened in that period which ultimately convinced me to start looking for some answers. I just wanted some proof that I was not losing my mind.

On the other hand, my life was getting better and better by the day. I loved working in the marine industry, and I loved the people I worked with. I was happy living on my yacht, and I was not single anymore. I was spending every weekend with my daughter in that beautiful environment, and I can say I was quite happy again.

Two or three nights per week, I spent in the company of my new girlfriend, having dinner together and trying to know each other on all levels, as two young adults do. There were many things we found in common, and I was always looking forward to our time together. She was a talented cook, we both loved music and good wine, and during dinners we used to have long conversations about everything and nothing.

I am a storyteller, and Diane was a good listener. Without me realising, I started talking about the more recent strange night events I was witnessing on the yacht while on my own, sharing my frustration of not being able to understand what really was going on, when, surprisingly, she came up with a suggestion that made sense to me. She encouraged me to seek outside help and have those faded memories of mine checked out.

This idea stayed with me for a while, and one day I found in the phone book the number of an organisation that was researching this very subject. As my frustration didn't go away, one day I picked up the phone and made that call. That very same afternoon, I met one of the research group members who came to meet me on the yacht. We talked a lot until late in the evening, and as a result of our conversation were several regression hypnosis sessions that followed, and the extraordinary stories which surfaced from my own suppressed memories.

I wrote several of those stories some time ago. They still fascinate me. I never, ever thought such experiences were stored in my subconscious, and yet there they were. Unfortunately, the ultimate result was that far more questions were raised than answers surfaced. Very frustrating!

I decided to ignore, at least try to ignore, what was happening on that front, and I was successful for a good period of time. I kept in touch with Don of course, and from time to time we called each other on the phone to chat on the subject or just say "hello." He was always willing to listen to my stories and try to give me advice if he could.

One day, he called me to let me know that Professor John Mack was in Sydney and was going to hold a seminar in the city on the subject of the phenomenon of alien abduction. Don asked me if I was interested in coming. He sparked my curiosity of course, and one evening we met downtown and took part in that seminar.

I was very impressed by Professor Mack. I found him extremely intelligent, well-spoken, and clear-minded. He had all the credentials of course: American psychiatrist, writer, professor, and head of the Department of Psychiatry at Harvard University Medical School. In 1977, John Mack won the Pulitzer Prize for his book *A Prince of Our Disorder* on T. E. Lawrence (Lawrence of Arabia).

As he presented to the audience, he came across this subject when commissioned by the US Air Force to study cases of air force personnel who witnessed strange encounters with extraterrestrial craft and their occupants. The idea was for him to study and determine if those people were suffering from any psychological disorders. The results of his study concluded that the subjects were normal from a mental point of view, and in his professional opinion, those people were the subjects of real and unusual experiences.

Later on, captivated by the topic, he continued the study at his university, where he again concluded that the interviewed people were not affected by any mental disorder, but were genuine individuals who lived traumatic experiences. He became personally interested in this intriguing phenomenon and started researching for himself, travelling the world in the quest for truth.

At the seminar, he talked about a worldwide phenomenon which potentially affects millions of people from all walks of life. The seminar was very interesting and of course triggered in my mind a new wave of unanswered questions. Later, I spoke with Don about it and briefly told him the story of the sailing trip in the Danube Delta in the summer of 1986.

The story of the night when camping with Helen on the bank of the Old Saint George River, when I found myself paralysed with fear under a powerful beam of light and not feeling the weight of my body. I told him about the strange feeling I had the next day of not being able to talk with Helen about what happened, and also about the unexplained healing of my leg infection. As always, Don listened with patience, and at the end of my story, he asked me if I was interested in finding out what really had happened that night. I was more than interested to know the truth; there was no doubt about that.

Don suggested the use of regression hypnosis again as a tool, and I agreed to go ahead with it. He also suggested contacting a different hypnotherapist who he had known for a long time and was confident in his ability to help. That gentleman was a professional hypnotherapist who used to work for the Police Force, and after his retirement, he joined the research group they both were part of.

A couple of weeks later, Don and I met in Manly, a very trendy and popular suburb of Sydney, where we were about to meet the new hypnotherapist who was going to help me regain my well-hidden memories. Our host was living in an apartment block on the main street in Manly, facing the very popular promenade along the beautiful beaches of the

Pacific Ocean. That area has always been packed with tourists and locals as well.

Chris invited us inside his apartment where he was living alone. We had a chat for some time, talking about our common interests and other subjects, most of them connected with Chris's former professional activity during his years of employment in the Police Force. I liked that calm, older man, full of interesting stories. I didn't feel any emotional tension, and I had no reservations about telling him why I was there and what I wanted to find out from the regression I agreed to go through under his supervision.

Chris warned me that sometimes, no matter his efforts, the results could be disappointing, and I shouldn't give up the goal of revealing what happened, no matter the outcome. We were invited into his office, where, to my surprise, we found a lot of video and sound recording equipment. Quite a professional setup in my opinion, and I discovered that Chris was very handy handling it all. I was surprised to see him doing that. I had always thought that older people couldn't handle sophisticated electronic equipment, but Chris proved me wrong.

It took him a few good minutes to set everything up for recording, while we kept talking about various things. From my previous experience in regression hypnosis, it took initially two to three sessions until I could finally reach that deep state of relaxation which ultimately allows the recovery of suppressed memories to surface. I was curious how many times I would have to come and see Chris until I could remember what was hidden so well in my subconscious. One thing was for sure: without reaching a total state of deep relaxation, all efforts would be in vain.

It was not going to be easy, considering those recording devices pointing in my direction, but that was the main reason I was there after all, and I was determined to give it a go. Don took a seat at the back of the room while Chris started the process of calming me down. I could see from the beginning that Chris's methods were slightly different from the other hypnotherapist I had met, but there was no doubt that his way of doing it reached my mind more efficiently, or I just found him easier to talk with.

Approximately twenty minutes later, I started to recall the evening I wanted to remember. It was the evening when, just after sunset, Helen and I were fast asleep in our tent on the Old Saint George River's bank. We were both tired after a long travelling day, and I was in throbbing pain due to my leg infection.

Suddenly, something felt wrong. I just didn't know what. I needed to find out where that feeling was coming from by trying to turn my body to one side to have a look. Nothing. I tried again to roll over, and it felt like my body was not mine. I lived in it, but I couldn't control it. I was paralysed by a phenomenon I couldn't understand. It felt like my entire body was vibrating from head to toe. Then, the panic came. I tried to fight it with no success. Every cell of my body vibrated. I was scared, and more than that, I felt hopeless. Whatever was happening, it was not within my power to control it.

A blinding, strong light was hurting my closed eyes; it was that powerful! The strangest thing: I couldn't feel the weight of my body. I felt like I was floating just centimetres above the ground. My surprise was about to become even bigger. I had never experienced or expected this. I felt that I was being lifted slowly and steadily into the air. The lifting itself was somehow unnatural. There was no inertia in this movement. There was no gradual feel of the lifting. All, absolutely all, the cells in my body were moving at exactly the same time. I had never experienced that feeling before, at least I didn't remember it. It was so strange.

The lifting was controlled by small adjustments, in such a way that my body was always kept perfectly horizontal. I was so scared that I lost consciousness. For a few long minutes, even under hypnosis, I couldn't feel or see anything. It was blank. Chris, the hypnotherapist, sensed what had happened and asked me to go forward in my regression, to the next significant moment of the experience. This is the miracle of hypnosis; somehow that is possible, and our brain manages to respond to these sorts of commands.

And so, I found myself in a very dark environment. It was very hard to distinguish anything from my surroundings because of that darkness. I believe I was in a sitting position and looking forward through what appeared to be a very large porthole, a large round window of unbelievable transparency. When I came around from my state of shock, I realised that I was looking at cosmic space. The glossy, dark, and cold space, full of round gold, red, and orange dots. Some closer than others, some bigger, and some shinier than others. All frozen in infinity.

I was… among the stars. What a powerful sight! I was fascinated! My fear totally disappeared. That panorama displayed before my eyes was breathtaking. There was no sound and no movement. Just the glittering stars of the Universe. My eyes were wide open, and my mind amazed by that incredibly beautiful view. I didn't know where I was, but just by looking at that incredible sight, I didn't care. I felt I was part of it. The feeling of fear didn't make sense anymore; this was a different realm. I was overwhelmed… I was in awe!

Time lost its meaning in the face of infinity. Nothing mattered but that very moment. That was reality… and yet reality did change, and time was born again.

The stars in my field of view slowly started moving. The nearby ones were moving faster than the ones coming from deep space.

One by one, sliding through the Ether, we were rushing to follow the stars that had already disappeared out of my view before. It was as if I were looking straight up into the darkness of the night at glowing orbs falling from the heavens and passing by in their rush to meet the infinity. It was total silence. I didn't sense any sign of motion other than the visual one, and yet the craft I was flying in was accelerating fast. The slow-moving stars, in only a few seconds, became shining traces of light. My forward view was filling quickly with those beams of light, optically generated by their incredible relative speed. A few more seconds later, the entire porthole I was looking through was fully lit. The speed increased to an unimaginable level and, despite that, my body felt no effects. No "G" forces, no blackout, no vibration… nothing. A pure forward motion at an unimaginable rate of acceleration. The craft I was travelling in was defying the laws of physics I thought I knew.

I was looking in dismay at that strangely lit porthole when, without any warning, it suddenly darkened. I was trying to understand what had just happened, but the surprise overwhelmed my judgement. I concentrated my attention on the new environment displayed in front of me. There was almost nothing. Far, very far in the depths of the Universe, I could vaguely distinguish a few faintly lit stars, but they looked to be really, really far away. The only explanation I could come up with was that the starting point of my flight was somewhere inside a cluster of billions of stars. Flying through that cluster at that incredibly accelerated speed, my vision recorded the transformation of the traces into a fully, brightly lit porthole. Those initial strings of light were the stars in their relative motion. They didn't move; we did. Their immense number filled the porthole with their tracing reflections. Once out of that cluster, the darkness of the Ether took over my view and surrounded me and the craft completely. It was incredible!

Time lost its meaning again. There was nothing to relate to. No point of reference… nothing. The darkness was almost complete, and those minuscule dots appeared to be so far away that the Universe looked as if it had run out of visible matter. I was desperately trying to find something to look at other than that immensity of nothingness. I could feel the fear starting to sneak into my mind again.

At that point, somewhere in the middle of the porthole, a round, pale source of light came to my attention. It appeared out of nowhere and slowly, very slowly, was getting closer in my view. For some strange reason, I had the impression that the craft I was travelling in was chasing it. The trajectory of that object, whatever it was, wasn't a straight line, and any slight deviation of its flight was immediately followed by its chaser. They both looked to be travelling in the same direction, with the difference that the chaser was slowly catching up.

This game continued for a long time. The object we were following was getting closer and closer. Its dimensions grew larger and larger in my view with every minute that passed. I could see by now that it was an artificial construction, round in shape, with no visible lights, but a very weak type of glow. It was dark grey, metallic-looking in colour, its surface flat but covered in what I could see from a far distance were fine striations of irregular forms and shapes.

The closer the craft I was travelling in came to that object, the bigger it appeared in my view, and the more details I could observe. I couldn't stop myself noticing that the object I was looking at was enormous in size. How big it was proved difficult to appreciate, but when the craft I was in got fairly close, its overall dimensions were by far bigger than my field of view, limited by the porthole I was looking through, and its image continued to grow.

At this stage, I could see better that those fine striations I had noticed before were now some type of protuberances resembling an industrial estate as seen from above. The velocity at which we were approaching the surface of that object was still very high. That metallic, irregular, industrial-looking surface was coming fast towards us. I became worried that we would crash into it, and yet we were not slowing down. I couldn't understand what the hell was going on.

I keep saying "we" because, in my mind, I assumed that there was somebody controlling the craft. Due to the interior darkness surrounding me, I was not able or maybe intentionally not allowed to see the interior of the craft, but somehow I assumed that someone was piloting it. Well, whoever was at its controls wasn't slowing it down.

Those metallic structures with the appearance of an industrial estate were now getting bigger and bigger, clearer and clearer to see. My initial worries had by now transformed into panic. My body became extremely tense, my muscles stiff. I was looking in terror at that enormous metallic structure approaching us very fast. My arms and legs were pushing my body into the armchair I was sitting in. In horror, I turned my head to one side, waiting for the impact. I didn't have the courage to look forward anymore.

My breathing was heavy, and under hypnosis I could hardly talk. I just couldn't understand why we were not slowing down. We were so close to that immense structure and, as in the worst nightmare, it wouldn't stop growing. At this stage of the hypnosis, I was extremely agitated, and Chris was trying his best to calm me down. I couldn't even look directly at what was happening; it was that frightening.

At the very moment when I was expecting the impact, the unexpected happened. Some huge structured triangular arms started moving outwards, creating a large opening in front of us. I was mind-blown! It was the last thing I expected. The craft flew straight through the middle of it into an enormous cavity. Even during the crossing of that opening, I noticed in stupor how those gigantic triangular gates were already closing behind us. That was unimaginable!

My initial terror transformed into exaltation. I just didn't expect that to happen. Under hypnosis, I couldn't stop shouting. I kept saying: "… I am in! … I am in! … I am in! … I can't believe it… I am in!" My breathing was still very heavy, but this time it was not because of fear but pure exaltation. Where was I? What the hell was that? Whatever it was… it was enormous!

The size of that new environment took my breath away. My mind wouldn't believe my eyes. I was looking through that porthole, trying to make sense of the things I was seeing.

The craft was flying in a straight line in the centre of what appeared to be an immense cylindrical cavity. Because of the darkness, I wasn't able to see all the way to the end of it. I could instead see its lateral walls, the ones we were flying parallel with. There was very little light in that environment, just enough to distinguish the similar type of protuberances which looked like the roofs of factories, part of an industrial complex. There were no movements of any kind and no apparent lighting of any kind; everything was still and silent.

The craft flew for minutes through the middle, passing the same dark grey metallic surface which looked like a dead industrial world. It was a strange feeling. It was a frozen, silent world. Nothing I could imagine or was accustomed to. Not having a reference point made it difficult to determine its size, but nevertheless it was enormous; something my imagination couldn't comprehend as possible. My eyes were eagerly looking for things I could recognise or relate to, but found nothing.

After a few good minutes of flying through the centre of the cylindrical structure, I observed that we were approaching a dark, enormous, vertical wall. My mind suddenly recognised the same scenario of flying too fast, getting too close, and the danger of crashing into it. That feeling proved founded when the craft didn't show signs of slowing down. The fear returned, and the history repeated. At the very moment when I was expecting the imminent impact, the same type of very large structured triangular mechanical arms opened in front of the craft and closed without a sound once we had passed through. Amazing! All was done in silence and with extraordinary precision.

We had just entered a second section of what I believed to be the same immense artificial structure in the shape of a cylinder. Flying through the middle again proved to be pretty much the same experience as the first one: the frozen stillness of those industrial constructions, engulfed in silence and darkness.

After minutes of travel through the centre of the second section of that gigantic cylinder, we approached the third perpendicular round, dark metallic partition wall. We were let through by the same type of huge triangular mechanical arms, which closed behind our passing.

The craft flew through two enormous cylindrical compartments and, after successfully crossing the third partitioning vertical wall, slowly came to a full stop. That was the first stop I had witnessed from the moment I was taken on board. I didn't initially understand the reason for its stopping. The only thing I could do was look outside the craft through the porthole, as I had done throughout the entire journey, and try to find the answer.

The darkness and the absolute silence were the same. We were floating, still, in the same type of cylindrical structure which appeared to be as big as the other two sections. There was a difference this time though. While I was looking straight ahead, trying to reach the other end, instead of seeing the darkness of the depth or perhaps even the fourth massive vertical metallic wall, I saw, with surprise, a large area densely covered in lights. They were all green in colour, resembling quite closely a city seen from a considerable height. I was not mistaken. It was easy to distinguish streets and building blocks in various directions and shapes.

Two things sparked my curiosity: there was no traffic or traffic lights on the streets, and nothing else was moving around as would happen in our cities. The city's lights were greenish in colour and still. A strange feeling took over me. I was fascinated by that sight. I was trying to imagine who was living down there, and I still couldn't understand why we were stopped so high up in the darkness, above that intriguing city, at the far end of that immense cylindrical megastructure. It seemed to me that we were waiting for some type of clearance to land from an unknown traffic controller. It felt strange because I couldn't see any traffic of any kind or any other type of movement at all.

It didn't take long after having these thoughts before the craft started moving again. Nothing could prepare me for what followed next. Slowly, the craft began descending towards that greenish illuminated city. My surprise became almost a painful frustration when I realised that the craft I had been taken into was not descending towards its landing target in the way I was expecting.

I am a licensed pilot myself. I have piloted, through the years, several types of aircraft and have been around airports and aviation in general for more than two decades. I was fascinated to see how that craft was performing very strange manoeuvres on its way down to the designated landing site. It was not manoeuvring to land like a plane and wasn't even descending directly like a helicopter. It was losing altitude in a very curious way, performing very large swings left and right, front and back. Strangely, it behaved similarly to a leaf falling from a tree down to the ground. What a strange way! And yet that wasn't the strangest thing.

Soon after the beginning of its curious descent, I started feeling the effect of inertia again. Throughout the entire flight, as I mentioned before, I hadn't been affected by such a thing. That craft accelerated to incredible speeds, changed direction multiple times while following that immense cylindrical structure, and ended up at a full stop just after crossing the third enormous vertical wall from its interior, and yet my body hadn't been affected in any way.

From the beginning of its descent towards the green city, the situation changed dramatically. Every swing in any direction pushed my body in the opposite sense, and I will be honest, that was very painful. My body was thrown from one side to the other quite violently, and I believe only some form of special harness or other type of restraint was holding me in my seat. The combination of pain and frustration made me angry. I was frustrated because I couldn't understand why we were descending in such a chaotic way. I was also in pain due to the rapid changes in direction and the "G" forces my body was exposed to.

For the first time during this experience, I started talking with someone. I have no memory of who I was talking to, but it was most likely the pilot or possibly the pilots. In my ignorance, I was trying to guide them to the landing site in the way I considered direct. The lights of the city were coming and going in my view through the porthole, and that frustrated me intensely. As a pilot, I had to align my aircraft with the runway and, by adjusting the airspeed and controlling the roll and pitch, landing was a fairly straightforward thing to do. Their manoeuvres and such an unconventional approach flight path were causing me pain. I was trying to shorten my discomfort by talking to them. I don't remember receiving an answer, but it became clear to me that the flight path had good reason to be the way it was. I was not in my world; I was in theirs. It looked like different rules applied there. The things I had witnessed in this amazing trip so far reminded me that I was not in a position to judge what was right or wrong, what was normal or not.

Hard to say what happened next. Very probably, I passed out. How long I was out, I can't say. When I came around and opened my eyes, I was no longer in the same place. The only similar thing was the darkness. I was lying down in a horizontal position, looking at a source of light similar to the one you would see at the dentist. It was a green light source in front of me, probably three metres away. I found that type of light very calming. It was quite possible that was its initial purpose by design.

Behind that light, I could see a few silhouettes walking around in silence. I found it very hard to distinguish what they were doing or how they really looked. I was not scared, and more importantly, I was not in pain anymore. I was just curious what was going on and what I was doing there. I discovered that I couldn't move, but that didn't bother me that much. I believe the green light had something to do with that. It was doing its job.

I concentrated my attention on those silhouettes behind the light, who looked busy doing something. I had no idea what. From time to time, one by one, they came close to where I was to take a look at me. Those beings were not like us. Their bodies looked fragile and thin. Because of the darkness, I couldn't see many details, but the most striking thing was their faces. They had large heads with small triangular faces, large dark eyes in a slanted position, thin noses and small mouths with very thin lips. They looked very serious and showed no facial expressions at all. I couldn't read anything on their faces whatsoever.

What was interesting was the way they approached me and looked at me. I noticed that those beings had very thin necks compared with the size of their heads and probably a much higher mobility in moving them. I found that they had a very unique way of tilting their heads in close proximity to whatever they wanted to look at. That was most intriguing. They came very close to my face, leaned their bodies over to be nearer, and then tilted their heads to one side for an even better look. We don't do that; we look straight. They didn't. I had the feeling that the tilting move could be a sign of curiosity and possibly a sign of care or affection. I couldn't be sure, and I didn't find that scary; just unusual.

Their dark eyes were the most expressive feature of their faces. Difficult to describe the feeling of looking straight into them. That was a type of connection between two different worlds. A universal silent language was doing the communication without the need to talk. It was an instant exchange of information where sentiments were totally ignored. A new type of existence I never imagined existed.

For a good period of time, I felt a strange vibration being applied in certain areas of my lower abdomen. It wasn't painful; just unusual. I wasn't told the purpose of what they were doing. I just accepted and tolerated it. Very probably, it was some form of scanning or perhaps a type of non-intrusive therapy. I didn't know. It was definitely concentrated in the navel area and later a little lower. All I knew was that I didn't feel any discomfort and that was good enough for me.

Their multiple approaches right next to my face gave me the impression that they cared and were comforting. It appeared to me that they were trying to make sure I was alright during their intervention or whatever that was. The multiple types of vibration I was feeling were concentrated in the abdominal area and, as I mentioned before, were not painful but unusual for my understanding, especially because I was not told the reason for them.

That situation changed soon. The vibrations stopped after a while and, to my surprise, I felt my legs being moved apart. Their area of interest changed, and I didn't like their new choice. I considered that as an intrusion into my privacy, and furthermore, to have that done without me being consulted. My thoughts appeared to have been read, and almost immediately, the green light from above my head changed to a strong orange one and, as a result, I lost consciousness.

What happened during the rest of that intervention I have no idea. For me, the time passed in a complete blackout. I would only like to believe that whatever happened, I was not supposed to know or remember, not even in a subconscious way. I have no doubt there was a good reason for that, and I would like to believe it was partly for my benefit too. I am certain of one thing: my leg infection was gone. When my awareness came back, I found myself in a sitting position, looking through the same porthole I had looked through during the first stage of that trip. I felt more comfortable somehow, knowing that I was back in the same craft that brought me inside that enormous cylindrical artificial structure.

I couldn't figure out what I was looking at outside the porthole. There was something I had never seen before. I was looking at some sort of fog… some form of clouds made of I couldn't tell what. Whatever those clouds were made of, it was not a solid material. As a whole, it looked like a cave, roughly carved into a round shape, out of a strange substance that didn't look solid but rather like a very dense fog, brownish in colour. Not having any point of reference whatsoever, it was impossible to determine its size in diameter. It could have been anywhere from a few hundred metres to maybe a couple of kilometres wide. One thing I knew for sure: it was the first time in my life I had seen such a thing.

My attention was caught when the craft started moving through it. It accelerated slowly until it reached a steady speed, and for what appeared to be ten to fifteen minutes, it flew straight through the middle of it. Even more surprising was that what I had initially thought was a cave proved to be a very long, winding tunnel, channelling us in every direction possible. Up and down, turning left and right in large and sometimes very steep curves in impossible-to-predict directions. Again, there were no physical effects on my body, and yet it was very hard to follow with my eyes the continuous and unexpected changes in direction. There was nothing geometrical about that strange tunnel other than its rough, foggy lateral walls and its imperfect round cross-section.

I fought hard not to pass out from motion dizziness when suddenly the craft came out of it. What happened next was so unexpected it took my breath away. Just outside the tunnel, my eyes caught sight of what appeared to be not one but two spacecraft, literally floating next to each other. The two craft were identical, and just by looking at their shape, I realised I had never, ever seen such a design for what appeared to be a flying machine.

There was nothing aerodynamic about their construction. They were triangular, with one of the corners presumably being the front, and the opposite side of the triangle the back. Their bodies were fairly thick, and the sides of those strange-looking craft were full of openings that were most likely rectangular windows. Each one had, on top and positioned towards the end, a vertical triangular stabiliser fin. That was also fairly thick, and it was hard to believe it presented any aerodynamic advantage. Both spacecraft were unlit, with no navigation lights or anything similar you would expect to see on a flying craft. They looked as though they were simply parked there, waiting to be used later.

Without a reference point, it was impossible for me to decide how big they were. I could only guess they were fairly large: between 100 and 150 metres in length, 10 to 15 metres thick, and 30 to 50 metres tall from their base to the top of the stabiliser fin. They appeared to be far more technologically advanced than any flying craft I had ever seen. I couldn't have imagined I would be given the opportunity to witness such a sight, and in such a location. The surprise was so intense and so unexpected. It was the first time I could see what I had only been guessing, how the craft I was travelling in possibly looked.

Unfortunately, the time those two spacecraft were in my view was very short. We were in motion, and the opportunity to see them was limited. The porthole I was looking through had a wide angle of sight, and that was the only reason that in such a short period, I was still able to notice all those interesting and surprising details.

I could hardly restrain my excitement, and yet the next thing that caught my attention was far more unforgettable. From the darkness of the tunnel we had been flying through before, and after I lost sight of the two out-of-this-world spacecraft, I turned my eyes forward. The most magnificent and unforgettable panorama was in front of me: ... The Universe !!! ... Wwwhhhaaauuuuu !!! What a view! How can I describe it in words? I honestly believe it is impossible. I wouldn't do it justice.

Unbelievably magnificent beauty. All of that would not even come close to the sensation of pure visual euphoria I witnessed. Nothing, absolutely nothing beautiful I have seen before, in any context, will ever compare with the splendour of the Universe. The purity, the diversity in shapes and colours of the galaxies, the immense number of stars floating in infinity, the glossy black of the Ether, it is breathtaking. I sincerely believe this is the ultimate experience a human being could dream of. It was that overwhelming. I was in awe.

We were flying among the stars in a curved trajectory. It was even more impressive that way. The Universe was showing off its splendour while I was on my way to be returned home. I blacked out…

The next thing I knew proved to be so different. All the euphoria was gone. I was unable to move, I couldn't feel the weight of my body, and I was very, very scared. I felt myself being lowered onto the ground, and when I finally managed to open my eyes and turn my head, I discovered with enormous relief that I was in the darkness of my tent, with Helen fast asleep right next to me. I didn't remember anything at all other than those last few minutes of that nightmare, and I lived in this state until the evening I met Chris.

I believe everything in life has its own timing. Maybe for me, that day was the time to remember what really happened on that night on the bank of the Old Saint George River, and the trip out of this world. What a surprise that was.

The End.

Epilogue

After the hypnosis session finished, we spent some time just talking about the events that came back to the surface from my well-hidden memories after so many years. The content of those memories was so surprising to me. I just couldn't imagine all that. Far too many things took me by surprise; things far beyond my realm of imagination.

Later in the night, Don and I said "goodbye" to Chris and went for a short walk on the beautiful promenade of Manly, along the beaches of the Pacific Ocean. I was still amazed by what had just come out of my suppressed memories, and I was trying to make sense of the entire story. Don was listening to me in silence, as he always did, without interrupting me. Time flew, and when we realised it was getting close to midnight, we decided to end our walk, pick up our cars, and go home.

Just before saying "goodbye" to each other, Don said:

"– Do you know, Victor, that a similar cylindrical space structure was photographed by the Russians a few years ago?" I couldn't believe what I was hearing.

"– They sent a space probe on a mission aimed for Mars," he added. "That probe was named *Phobos 2*. They flew it to Mars and, just before approaching the planet, they lost contact and never heard from it again. The curious thing is that the last two photos that probe sent to Earth were taken next to one of Mars's moons, called Phobos. Both photos showed something that appeared to be a cylindrical structure, which looked artificial, and was estimated by their specialists to be approximately 25 kilometres long and two kilometres in diameter. This information about the sighting was kept secret until the fall of Communism, when a Soviet female cosmonaut, Marina Popovich, revealed what really happened with that lost mission and presented those two photos to the world."

Don's story haunts me to this day. Was that possible? Did I visit that enormous structure? I really don't know. I have memories of seeing it from outside and remembering its interior. Had I imagined it?

No! … I might have an imagination, but I couldn't imagine the unimaginable!

Chapter 5:
Someone Watching From Above …

True story.

Geraldton Airport.

West Coast, Australia.

The morning sky was covered by low, dark grey clouds, tumbling fast like countless and frightening waves of a stormy ocean. Pushed by gusty winds, they were leaving behind cold and heavy rain. The fast-moving curtains of raindrops falling from the heavens made it difficult to see anything through. Inside the regional airport, the few passengers were waiting in silence to find out if their flights were still going ahead because of those unfriendly weather conditions.

For me, it was the end of a five-day business trip. I was returning from the desert down to the coast, and I was ready to go home. The weather had been bad from the beginning and hadn't improved throughout that long and monotonous trip. In that part of the world, it was not unusual to experience this type of cold weather front, usually associated with low atmospheric pressure. Formed over the moisture-saturated Indian Ocean, it had moved eastwards, bringing rain and howling gales for almost five consecutive days. The City of Geraldton, positioned on the west coast of the continent, right next to this immense body of water, was receiving the full blow of that weather event.

Looking through the dense curtains of falling rain, I spotted a landing passenger plane at the other end of the airdrome. With a bit of luck, that was the one that would take me home. It touched down gently on the main runway and taxied slowly to its parking bay in front of our terminal.

Soon, the pilots stopped its engines, and we were invited to board the aircraft and take our seats. I was still wondering what the chances were of departing. It was cold, and I was wet. In the short distance between the terminal and the plane, we had to walk outside into the open. The rain didn't spare us, and in such a short walk we were drenched.

I took my seat by the window, somewhere in the middle of the cabin, and got comfortable. I looked outside, hoping to see the rain slowing down a little. Outside, the water droplets were hitting the plastic window and quickly running off it just in time to make room for the next wave, chasing each other over and over again. That image was hypnotic. The plane started to roll slowly on the taxiway, getting ready to take us to the skies. I closed my eyes and let my thoughts run free.

For some unknown reason the date came to my mind; it was the first of June. The first day of winter in the Southern Hemisphere, the official opening day of the ski season in Australia.

My memory went back to an event that took place several years ago. Soon, I understood why. Two details were the same: the date and the weather. A strange sentiment of nostalgia invaded my soul. I allowed my mind to go back to that long weekend when a good friend of mine, Mark, and I decided to take advantage of those three free days off. We had planned to fly a plane to the skiing fields of the Snowy Mountains on the first day of the long weekend. We were going to ski on the second day and return home on the last one.

Mark and I knew each other from Sydney Aviation College, the flying school we both attended. That's where we became friends. We shared a passion for flying and, as we later discovered, we both loved skiing too. As an irony of life, we happened to be single parents during that period, and probably that was one more thing we had in common, which might explain our friendship. We were both in pretty much the same situation.

We flew several times together during our training, sharing the cockpit and the flying time. We took turns flying the plane from the left seat (the pilot-in-command seat), and by doing that we were not only making the long navigation flights cheaper but, at the same time, safer. Mark owned a Piper Cherokee Warrior, a four-seater aircraft, and naturally we decided to use his plane for our snow adventure.

As our planned flight had to include a stop for refuelling, we chose Wangaratta, a regional airdrome in New South Wales, which was positioned about halfway to our destination. After filling up the fuel tanks, we agreed to change seats, sharing the flying time. I offered to pilot the plane first, land in Wangaratta, refuel, and let Mark finish the trip in Jindabyne, the mountain town with its airport nearby. We had landed on that airdrome on another occasion when we travelled together to Melbourne in Victoria to witness the

Avalon International Airshow. The small Jindabyne Airdrome has a relatively short and unsealed runway, and it was wiser to let Mark land there, as he was more familiar with it than I was.

The meteorological conditions on the day of our departure were great, we couldn't have wished for better, and our three-and-a-half-hour flight went smoothly and uneventfully. We were happy to do what we both loved, and we were even more excited for the coming day when we were planning to enjoy the snow and the beautiful views of the Snowy Mountains. We checked the ski conditions on the internet and found that the slopes were already covered by fresh snow, and skiing was promised to be pretty damn good.

Once in the air, as per our routine, we helped each other with the navigation tasks and, as usual, in between we chatted about everything and nothing. During our conversation, Mark mentioned that he was aware of another plane leaving from Bankstown (our base airport in Sydney) that was going in the same direction. Same as us, only two people on board. One of the pilots was a mutual friend we both knew from the flying school, and the other pilot was a young man neither of us had met before. Mark also knew that plane and the call sign of the aircraft they were flying.

Approaching Canberra's controlled airspace, as always, we monitored the radio traffic between the air traffic controllers and the other aircraft in the area. Mark and I had planned our route together and decided to keep it simple. We intentionally avoided controlled airspaces, especially the one around Canberra, the capital city. As required by regulations, we had to monitor that specific radio frequency, which is how we heard our friend flying the other plane, requesting clearance to pass through. They were granted the clearance, which told us they were already ahead and would arrive in Jindabyne first.

After bypassing Canberra's airspace, our plane was getting close to the mountains. We admired that beautiful panorama from the air. The terrain was rising higher and higher, and with every minute that passed, the view became more captivating. Covered at lower levels by dense eucalyptus woods, the mountains had their tops shining with white snow. They looked magnificent from up there, and we could be certain now that we would have enough snow for the following day of skiing.

Finally, in the early hours of the afternoon, our plane was circling the Jindabyne airdrome. As the sky was still clear of clouds and there was no wind, we had no difficulty locating it and landed smoothly on its runway. The crew of the other plane was waiting for us nearby. They had parked their aircraft and guided us to do the same. Once the shutdown procedures were finished, Mark and I went to meet them on the tarmac.

We shook our friend's hand, and he in return introduced the young man we knew nothing about. His name was Flavius. He was young, tall, athletic, very good-looking, with a sincere smile on his face that made us like him from the very first moment. Meeting him, I had the strong impression that I had seen him before, and I was right.

It didn't take long for me to remember. In the morning, before our departure to the snowfields, Mark and I were inside the flying school checking the weather on an aviation forecast website and working on our flight plan for the trip. A young couple was just about to enter the building. Involuntarily, they caught my attention.

I saw them parking their car in the carpark, and once out of the vehicle, they hugged and kissed each other goodbye. I had a good look at them both. Through the large glass door at the front of the building, my attention was drawn to what looked like an idyllic movie scene. The couple was glamorously saying goodbye to each other in front of a beautiful late-model convertible sports car. It was something you don't see every day. It was actually a very nice scene. They were young, in their mid-20s, good-looking, elegantly dressed. Next to them, a new-model Mercedes. I realised instantly that the guy I was admiring at that moment was Flavius.

The surprises didn't stop there. After a few minutes of chatting next to the two planes, all four of us collected our things from inside the aircraft and called a taxi. The cab arrived quickly, and we left the airdrome for a half-hour ride to the ski resort of Thredbo, where we planned to find accommodation. We hadn't booked anything in advance, and considering it was a long weekend and the ski season had just opened, we were worried it might be tricky to find somewhere to stay. Flavius solved the problem with ease. Once in the taxi, he took a laptop out of his bag and, while the rest of us admired the winding, snow-covered mountain road, he searched online for accommodation. Even before we reached the resort, he had found what he was looking for and offered a few options. Our fears were left behind, and we chose a small apartment with four beds in a pretty villa somewhere in the snow-covered, postcard-like ski resort of Thredbo.

By the time the taxi dropped us in front of our villa, it was already dark. I was struck by the beauty and magic of the winter atmosphere in the mountain town where we had just arrived. Everything around us was covered in fresh, soft snow. The warm glow of the streetlights harmonised perfectly with the peaceful fall of large snowflakes gently drifting from the sky. It was a beautiful welcome from nature to our small group of tired travellers. We checked into the villa, dropped our things in the room, and soon went out again to find a place for dinner.

Walking through the narrow streets of Thredbo that night, snow gently falling from above and breathing in the crisp, pure mountain air, was magical. In the town centre, plenty of people like us were either looking for a place to eat or simply enjoying a stroll in the snow. We found a small, cosy restaurant and had dinner surrounded by other diners, families, groups of friends, couples, all enjoying that beautiful winter night in the mountains.

After dinner, we were too tired even to consider staying out. We walked back to the villa, chatting and planning for the coming day. All four of us were keen skiers, looking forward to a full day on the slopes. So, we decided to get to bed early and rest. Easy said than done. Unfortunately, we behaved like kids waiting for Santa Claus on Christmas Eve, full of curiosity and excitement. Because of the anticipation, we just couldn't fall asleep and, without realising it, we started chatting. As Flavius sat slightly apart from the circle, he became the target of most of our questions. We were curious about where he was from, given his unusual name, and about his passion for flying. His story captured our attention from the start, and we ended up listening in silence like a bunch of kindergarten children at storytime. The irony was that he was the youngest among us four.

Flavius told us he was born in Spain, Europe, into a family with a very colourful history. From what he said, his mother disappeared from his life early on, leaving him uncertain whether she was dead or alive. He grew up being raised solely by his father, who was somehow connected to the underworld of the country and eventually ended up in prison for a long period. During his teenage years, Flavius was in the care of the Spanish Government, growing up in an orphanage. Once he was on his own, he worked as an IT technician for a couple of years, during which he became a specialist in programming and all things computer-related. Attracted by adventure, he decided to emigrate to Australia as soon as he turned twenty-one.

Arriving in Sydney, he successfully established his own IT company, which he transformed within a few years into a profitable business. By then, he was employing others, had married, and could finally afford to fulfil his childhood dream of flying. He also had plans, seeking council approval to build a state-of-the-art house for himself, his young wife, and his future children. Because of his business and personal success, and his challenging and colourful childhood, he was often invited by government social workers to give motivational speeches at various children's institutions similar to the one he had grown up in. Flavius spoke sincerely yet modestly about his achievements. He loved sharing his short but accomplished life story, and I'll admit it, he had every reason to be proud.

The following day proved to be fantastic. Early in the morning, we hired our skiing equipment, bought lift passes, and, without needing encouragement, headed up to the mountain tops. The weather and snow conditions were excellent. The shining sun, crisp mountain air, and physical exertion soon gave us healthy red tans on our faces. The surrounding mountains, all covered in snow, the deep blue cloudless sky, and the feeling of ultimate freedom from skiing down the slopes made that day unforgettable. We were lucky to discover that our ski abilities were quite similar, which meant we could ski together, making it far more enjoyable than being alone.

At lunchtime, we stopped halfway up the mountain at a busy ski lodge to eat, rest our legs, and quench our thirst with a couple of beers. Many others were there doing the same. Sunlight on the snow, music, full stomachs, and beer gave the day a perfect winter holiday feel. What else could four young, healthy men wish for?

When evening came, we were tired and very hungry. A shower and the nice feel of dry, warm clothes gave us enough energy to go out for dinner. We went to a different restaurant down in the village, but the relaxed, happy vibe was the same. Being the last night in the mountains, nobody really wanted to go to bed after dinner. The boys wanted to hit a bar for more drinks. I promised I would meet them there later. I knew the place they were talking about, we had passed it the night before, and it looked popular, definitely the place to be.

I didn't intend to drink too much that night. The following morning, we were leaving the mountains and heading home. It was my turn to fly first, and I wanted to be in top mental and physical shape. The weather wasn't looking promising, and having a hangover would not have helped.

During dinner, however, I somehow struck up a conversation with two young women sitting close to our table. By the end of the meal, I invited them to a nightclub, and they accepted. I knew I was aiming high, but it was worth a try. The girls were pretty, and I was a single man. Once we finished eating, the three of us said goodbye to the others and headed out. The nightclub was packed and very noisy, and an hour later my dancing adventure ended with the girls deciding to call it a night and go to bed. No hard feelings on my part, I knew I had been overoptimistic. It's hard, if not impossible, to get anywhere without a wingman.

As promised, I went to meet my friends at the bar. The atmosphere was electric. Drinks were strong, the music loud, women everywhere, and it didn't take long to see that most of them were noticing just one man: Flavius. I had never seen anything like it. I don't know what Flavius had done to draw them in, but they swarmed around him like bees to honey. I took a moment to observe, and I concluded that Flavius somehow embodied exactly what they wanted. With his cheerful personality and striking appearance, he was the man of the night. He engaged with them, mostly responding to their advances, but never went further, remaining neutral while still at the centre of female attention. It was the mystery of women at its best. Somehow, by not showing any personal interest, he made them try harder, competing with each other while the other men in the bar could only dream of such success. That night, women wanted him, and men wanted to be him.

At closing time, we left the bar, and Flavius came with us. He hadn't chosen any of those women, though there was no doubt he could have if he'd wanted to. Late that night, the party over, back in our room, we started chatting about the day just finished. The boys jokingly called me the Casanova of the evening because I had left the restaurant with those two women. I didn't want to claim that title without merit, so I explained what had really happened. The true Casanova, of course, was Flavius. Any man would be proud to be associated with the name of the most successful man in the history of mankind. Flavius, however, said he wasn't interested. He loved his wife and wouldn't risk his marriage for the pleasure of a one-night stand with women he might never see again. Many might disagree with that, but Flavius stood firm in his belief.

Morning came. We got up early and immediately checked the weather. The aviation forecast didn't look promising. A low-pressure front was expected from the east, bringing low cloud, gusty winds, rain, and high turbulence. It was due to arrive around midday, but there was a fair chance to beat it if we departed as early as possible. We finalised our flight plans with the information we had and left our villa in Thredbo by taxi. The previous day had been one of the best skiing experiences I could remember; now it was time to go home.

At the airport, we enquired about fuel availability. The answer was not what we expected. We couldn't refuel there, we would have had to be members of the local flying club, which we weren't. I checked the fuel remaining in my tanks. The result wasn't too bad: approximately two hours of flying time remained, assuming normal conditions. If all went as planned, we would have enough fuel to reach Moruya, an airdrome on the coast, where we could refuel safely and continue to Sydney. I consulted Mark, and we decided to give it a go.

Flavius and our other friend didn't have this problem. Their aircraft was a newer generation with much more fuel-efficient engines, giving them plenty of fuel for the journey. Their plane was lighter and faster, equipped with modern digital navigation and control systems, and had the added advantage of autopilot, which later proved extremely useful.

Flavius started his engine, taxied his plane to the runway, lined it up, and took off first. A few minutes later, I did the same. It was my turn to fly, so I took the left seat in the cockpit, with Mark to my right. Our flight plan was to climb, clear the mountains, track east towards Moruya Airport, refuel there, swap seats, and continue north, following the coast all the way to Sydney. In theory, our first leg would take no more than an hour, leaving us with 60 minutes of fuel in reserve. Unfortunately, that proved true only in theory.

Not long after take-off, while still climbing, I noticed dense clouds on the horizon coming from the east. Within minutes, we were engulfed in them. At first, it wasn't too bad. I lost some forward visibility, but I could still see the ground beneath. I kept climbing, hoping to get above the cloud level, with occasional ground references in sight. That was legal under VFR (Visual Flight Rules) and safe for us and the aircraft.

Minutes later, our hopes were disappearing fast. The clouds thickened and darkened. The wind intensified, gusting unpredictably. I had to concentrate hard to keep the plane climbing while maintaining level wings and the calculated heading. A few minutes after that, we were already past the point of no return. My plane was completely inside the clouds, and I had lost all view of the ground, forcing me to fly on instruments only.

During our training, flying on instruments had been part of the curriculum. The reality, however, was that we had only three hours of instrument training, done under a plastic hood that blocked the outside view, in good weather, and under a qualified flight instructor who could take over if necessary. This time was real, unsimulated, as real as it could get.

The strong wind had turned into a storm, and our plane was being thrown mercilessly up and down like a small sailing boat battling a gale, fighting stubbornly to stay on course. We had flown in bad weather before, but never like this. During training, we had been warned this could happen, with advice to stay calm and, above all, keep the wings level as much as possible.

I checked my instruments. The altimeter showed 4,000 feet. I wasn't high enough. I had no choice but to keep climbing. The maps indicated elevations over 7,000 feet. I needed at least 1,000 feet above that to ensure we cleared the mountain peaks. The situation was extremely difficult, and I struggled to find an alternative. I considered returning to Jindabyne Aerodrome, but abandoned the idea almost immediately. Outside, I could see nothing but fast-moving grey clouds, likely stretching to the ground. Diverting to the nearest airdrome, Cooma, wasn't an option either. I couldn't risk descending blind and attempting to land on a mountain-surrounded runway I couldn't see.

I was left with only one plan: fly high, clear the mountains, keep the wings level, and follow the planned track to Moruya as best I could. Once there, pray for a miracle to allow a safe landing.

My eyes left the instrument panel and scanned outside. Nothing. Dark grey clouds surrounded the aircraft, and its fuselage shook violently with every rivet. I felt the chaotic movement, rolling left and right, climbing and descending like a twig on a mountain river rapid. I was still climbing blind. The conflicting information from my senses and the instruments became confusing. It was very hard to describe the terrifying feeling. In aviation, this phenomenon is called "spatial disorientation." It's what killed John F. Kennedy Jr., his wife, and his sister-in-law. Horrifyingly, he was flying the same type of aircraft as us when it happened.

I remembered the strong advice from our instructors: *"Don't trust your senses… they will betray you! Always trust the instruments… they will serve you well… keep your wings level and stay calm."* Easy to say when your life isn't hanging by a thread.

The engine was at full power, struggling when the angle of climb increased and over-revving when the nose dipped. Until now, the 150 HP Lycoming motor had been my only friend. The thought of gliding the aircraft in the storm toward dark mountain cliffs froze my heart. A painful sense of hopelessness paralysed me. I panicked. For a split second, I froze. I was scared. I sincerely thought it was the end. In that moment, I felt closer to heaven than ever before. I didn't know what to do or if it was even worth fighting.

Then I thought of God. Inexplicably, my will to fight returned. I didn't want to give up. I resolved to follow my training: *"Keep your wings level, fly straight, and solve problems one by one."* I was still scared, but now I felt hope.

My chain of thoughts was interrupted by the radio. After a few crackles, a transmission came through. It was Flavius.

It was his voice. He called us using the plane-to-plane VHF frequency, just to let us know he had climbed to 10,500 feet and his aircraft had emerged from the clouds. He could see the horizon again and the crystal-clear sky above. He told us that flying conditions were much better and gave his position: about 60 NM west of Moruya Airport. Hearing his voice through the headsets and the information he shared gave me an extra boost of hope. Now I knew exactly what I had to do. I had to keep climbing until we broke out of the clouds. According to him, that would happen at approximately 10,000 feet. Once out, we would have less turbulence and the horizon in sight. I would again be able to see up from down without relying on the artificial horizon on the instrument panel. I would be fully in control once more.

I followed Flavius's instructions and, minutes later, found he was entirely right. It was great to see the clear sky and to fly in relative safety. Unfortunately, the moment of relief didn't last long. I checked my watch for the time and immediately looked at the fuel gauges. As I feared, the tanks were very low. The headwinds brought by the storm, continuous full-power climbing, and likely extra distance flown due to drift had brought the fuel level dangerously low.

As the saying goes, "When it rains, it pours", our troubles were far from over. Looking outside, I noticed a thin layer of ice forming on the wings. That was really bad news. At 10,000 feet, the outside temperature was well below zero, and the air around the plane was full of icicles building up in layers over the wings, windscreen, and fuselage. We were now flying an iced aircraft, at risk of falling out of the sky due to the extra weight, reduced lift, and increased drag. It was not a good day.

It became clear that we needed to descend, both because of the icing and the lack of oxygen. We couldn't stay long at that altitude, yet we had no choice. Every minute that passed made our situation more critical: very low fuel, an iced aircraft at high altitude with insufficient oxygen, flying a track that could be off course due to drift, and an unknown position. While in the clouds, I maintained our direction using the compass only. I tried as hard as I could to hold the calculated heading, but without ground references, only God knew how far we had drifted. We could be miles from our intended track without any way of knowing.

A stroke of luck came. The plane's ADF (Automatic Direction Finder) sprang to life. We were within 40 NM of the Moruya NDB (Non-Directional Beacon), and the needle now indicated the correct direction to the airport. I banked the wings, changed course according to the ADF, and reassessed our situation. Reality was still grim. Fuel could run out any minute. Both tanks read nearly empty. I knew the gauges were inaccurate, but I didn't know in which way. The engine could stop at any moment, making my heartbeat race and my neck arteries pulse violently under the skin.

We were still flying at 10,500 feet, above dark, angry clouds, closing in on Moruya. Landing there could end our nightmare, but we first had to survive descending. Blindly descending through the clouds was almost suicidal. Mountain ranges stretched all the way to the ocean, where the runway was. I could fly a few more minutes east, past the airport, over the water, and only then descend to 500 feet above sea level. Perhaps visibility would be enough to see the shore and follow it back to the airport. But would the fuel last that long? I felt trapped. We were in God's hands again… and God was watching.

Flavius's voice came through the radio again, breaking my spiralling thoughts. He had landed his plane and was thinking of us. He only knew we were struggling with fuel and visibility. Looking at the sky, he identified two openings in the thick cloud layers. One was about five nautical miles south of the airport over the beaches, the other roughly 10 NM east over the ocean. He advised me to fly east, above the water, descend through that opening, then follow the shore back to land. He was right, that was the safest option, but my instincts warned me that our engine was running on fumes. I feared any extra mile could cost us the chance to reach the ground. Gliding wasn't an option; we could end up ditching in the ocean, unsure how far from the shore.

I scanned the sky through the windscreen. Thank God, I found them. Flavius had been right. The two holes were exactly where he said. My heart nearly leapt out of my chest. I banked the wings and turned the plane south, heading for the closest one. I didn't want to push our luck. With every second flying towards that miracle, my blood pressure rose, and my hands squeezed the controls tighter. We were close, but there were no guarantees. Every minute felt like an eternity.

With the engine still running, I finally reached the cloud opening. One of the most glorious moments of my life. It was breathtaking, perhaps the most amazing sight I had ever seen. Almost perfectly circular, the hole looked like a sci-fi time tunnel, its vertical walls made of giant white clouds. It seemed as if an imaginary hand had pushed the clouds aside just enough for us to fly through. From the top of that opening, at 10,000 feet, I could miraculously see all the way down to the beaches. Mountain vegetation to the west, golden sands, and the light blue ocean with white-capped waves. What a sight! What a chance I had, and I was determined to take it.

I slowly reduced engine power, gently pushed the control column down, and banked the wings, descending in a large spiral to the left, almost grazing the clouds with the fuselage. With every turn, the plane descended towards the tunnel's exit. Once out, life returned to view. As a bonus, the last loop positioned the aircraft facing the coastline to the north, directly aligned with Moruya Airport's runway. That glorious sight, which I had only dreamed of minutes before, was now right in front of me. I was overjoyed.

I made the required radio calls, idled the engine, lowered full flaps, and the landing gear touched down, rolling along the runway. At the end of the landing roll, I exited the main runway, taxied a few hundred metres, applied the brakes, and shut down the engine next to the fuel bowser. Finally, we were safe.

What a flight! What a day!

The Old Man from Heaven looked down on us and let us live to tell the story.

From that feeling of exaltation and gratitude, I suddenly remembered Flavius. He was the man who made it happen. Deep down, I knew his two radio transmissions had saved our lives. I looked around for his plane, for him, but I couldn't see either. He was gone.

He had flown ahead of us… he had flown into eternity.

I never saw Flavius again. He died a few months later in a motorcycle accident.

I heard that he had separated from his wife, who allegedly had been unfaithful, and that this may have somehow influenced his crash.

He was only 26 years old.

What bothers me most is that I never got the chance to say, "Thank you." This still upsets me and will continue to do so for the rest of my days. Every time I think of him and remember this story, I have a tear or two in my eyes.

Rest in peace, Flavius… and thank you.

I hope my story will give you justice.

The End.

Chapter 6:
A Stormy Night Over the Pacific

True story

Several years ago, I received an unusual present from my special lady, Valerie. She had bought me a small Māori amulet made of whale bone from her native New Zealand. According to the indigenous people, it was believed to protect whoever wore it while travelling over the oceans.

Valerie and I had been boating together for many years, spending most of our free time on either our sailing yacht or fishing boat. She considered that extra protection wouldn't hurt anyone, even if it was only psychological. I never imagined that one day her precious gift would perform its magic, saving my life, the lives of my companions, and our vessel.

Berowra Waters, Sydney

At the beginning of January 2016, a good friend of mine, Paul, suggested sailing his newly purchased yacht to Port Stephens. We were still in our Australian summer holiday, past the festive season, so his idea sounded fantastic.

The plan was to sail north along the coast, reach Port Stephens, enter the beautiful Nelson Bay, spend a few days there, and return by sea to Sydney, refreshed and ready to go back to work.

One early morning, Paul, my younger son Nicholas, and I loaded the yacht with provisions for a few days, water, fuel, spare clothes, and fishing gear, and left Berowra Waters

Marina, heading for the ocean. We faced a 25-nautical-mile trip through the interior waterways, expected to take the rest of the day. These waterways were familiar to us, the usual playground for short weekend boating trips throughout the year.

The Hawkesbury River system created a spectacular, Norwegian-fjord-like environment, guarded by modest mountains covered in eucalyptus forest. The winding river and mountains made sailing difficult, so we relied entirely on the diesel engine.

Late in the afternoon, we arrived at Broken Bay, where we could see the ocean in the distance. It was too late, and we were too tired to venture further. Instead, we veered right into Pittwater, a large, protected area separated from the Pacific Ocean by a narrow strip of land, the well-known Palm Beach. We anchored for the night in a picturesque and popular bay known as "The Sailor's Retreat." The preparation and long hours of motoring had taken their toll, and we were ready to rest. The waters were calm, but the sky was overcast, hinting at similar weather the following day.

Pittwater, Sydney

The second day of the sailing trip to Nelson Bay, Port Stephens

We were living the dream. Eager to reach our destination before sunset, we decided to leave at 06:00. Just before lifting the anchor from the sandy bottom of the bay, I checked the weather once more. The Bureau of Meteorology forecast was favourable. No warnings were in place; it promised an average rainy day with a S–SE wind at 15–20 knots, ideal for sailing north.

Paul's yacht was a Compass 28 sloop, a classic fibreglass hull with a full-length keel, giving excellent stability under sail. It wasn't fast, but it was steady and comfortable in rough conditions.

The first time I sailed it was only a few months earlier. Paul had asked me to help move his newly purchased yacht from Sydney Harbour, where the previous owner had kept it, to Berowra Waters. The weather that day was rough, and I questioned whether taking the boat into the ocean was a mistake. I worried about our safety, Valerie and my boys were with us. The closer we got to the Sydney Harbour Heads, the more concerned I became.

That area is notorious for large waves in certain conditions, especially with a southerly wind, as we had that day. Reluctantly, I decided to proceed cautiously, ready to turn back to Sydney Harbour if necessary. Slowly, I guided the yacht through the heads. To my relief, it handled the conditions extremely well. There had been moments when I almost turned back, but soon the yacht earned my trust. I sailed with only the jib up at the front. The hull and rigging weren't stressed, and the boat maintained 6–7 knots per hour. We were cold and wet from the gusty wind and spray, but the trip was exhilarating.

In the following months, Paul equipped his yacht with top safety gear: a brand-new inflatable tender and outboard motor, fire extinguishers, bilge pumps, new marine batteries, and a top-of-the-range EPIRB (Emergency

Position Indicating Radio Beacon). This device self-activates when in water, transmitting position to satellites for a search and rescue response. The day before our departure, I installed a new two-way 27-megahertz marine radio.

All the new equipment, combined with the solid construction of the hull and rigging, gave me the peace of mind I needed to go ahead with the trip.

In the morning of our departure for Port Stephens, while still in the Broken Bay area and before entering the ocean, I decided to organise the deck a little, just to make sure we would have a safe and comfortable trip. We lifted the inflatable tender out of the water and tied it up on top of the cabin. The holding ropes had quick-release knots, just to make it easy to launch back into the ocean in case of emergency. The outboard motor was secured on a special support mounted on the safety rails at the aft of the yacht. We tested the 27-megahertz radio and installed the EPIRB on its support bracket on the main cabin wall, handy, next to the entry hatch. We were wearing our personal life jackets, just in case. After all those preparations, we were on our way to Port Stephens.

The first three to four hours of the trip passed without any noticeable event. We just enjoyed the lazy movement of the boat among the waves, the sound of the wind whistling through the rigging, and the Latin music played through the cockpit speakers by the yacht's stereo system.

Unfortunately, the wind changed direction, and the weather conditions became worse than the forecast had suggested. To boost our speed, I decided to start the inboard diesel motor while keeping both sails, the main and the jib, up. All those efforts made the yacht reach a speed of 6 to 7 knots. I knew by then that reaching Nelson Bay before sunset would be a challenge. We were in very good spirits despite the light rain and the increased wind strength. The yacht was slowly but steadily reducing the distance to our destination. The waves were 2 to 2.5 metres high but well apart from each other, which made our boat feel very comfortable among them.

From time to time, groups of wild dolphins came to the surface right next to our hull, curious to check us out. It was a strange but invigorating feeling to see such beautiful and intelligent sea creatures so close to our boat. They showed off their swimming skills and, after only a few minutes of their company, left us in peace to make room for the next group of aquatic visitors.

Abeam Newcastle, somewhere around half the distance between Sydney and Port Stephens, Paul noticed that the main cabin had filled with thick black smoke. It was almost impossible to breathe or see anything inside. It wasn't difficult to discover the source. It was clear that something was wrong with our diesel motor. I stopped it right away and looked for the problem. By lifting the engine room cover, I noticed that the exhaust manifold, due to continuous vibrations, had detached itself from the engine block. Now, the exhaust smoke, instead of being channelled outside through the exhaust system, was filling the main cabin.

I asked Nick, my younger son, to take over the tiller and steer the yacht using sail power only. Paul and I started looking for a repair solution using only the few tools we could find on board. To reach the area where the exhaust manifold had fallen off, I had to dismantle the engine box and its sound insulation panels. It took me some time to do that. There was very little room to work in, but in the end, I managed to reattach the unbolted parts. We were lucky, there was no permanent damage. Only a few bolts had loosened until the exhaust manifold fell off. Dirty and sweaty, working in a very cramped space, I managed to re-bolt everything together. Luckily, I was used to this type of work from my own yacht diesel motor which was quite similar.

One and a half hours later, the diesel engine was happily running again. Meanwhile, the wind and waves had increased, and we were late for our daytime arrival into Nelson Bay.

Darkness came, and we were still 30 nautical miles away from our arrival. With the night came the storm as well, strong gusty winds, large waves, and heavy rain. I made the decision to lower the sails and run on the engine only. I didn't want to overstress the rigging and the hull of the yacht. The gusty and strong wind was dangerously leaning the vessel to port, and combined with the pounding of the powerful waves, could have caused the yacht to capsize.

I asked Paul to go out on deck and get the sails down. I remained at the tiller trying to keep the boat, as much as I could, with its bow into the wind. We had no other choice. Paul understood the seriousness of the situation and went to the bow to start the difficult task of getting the sails down. I watched him and realised that if he were washed into the ocean by a rogue wave, I would lose him forever. The darkness surrounding us was frightening, and I knew that by the time I grabbed a torch from inside the cabin and started looking, the chances of spotting him would be very small. The storm came fast and, with my mind busy worrying, I simply forgot to ask him to tie himself with a safety rope.

I watched Paul at the front of the boat in the difficult position of pulling the sails down while fighting to keep his balance. The yacht was climbing and descending, riding those aggressive waves courageously, while the higher ones broke over the deck, covering Paul in white foam and soaking him to the bone. It was dangerous, yet he ultimately succeeded in getting the sails down and securing them with ropes against the boom and the front safety rails.

We continued battling the stormy night, navigating by compass and the portable GPS Paul had. We were wet and very, very cold. For that reason, we took turns steering the yacht, and I noticed that Paul was doing very well for a man who hadn't spent much time on the water. He confessed to me that it was the first time he had witnessed such rough weather and that he was scared. I would be a liar if I didn't admit that I had moments of fear too. It was the impenetrable darkness and nature's fury that scared me as well.

I vividly remember, sometime during the night while the yacht was falling from the top of a large wave, spotting a big albatross on the port side of the boat, almost crushed by the plunging hull.

Frightened, it spread its large wings and desperately beat the water several times. The bird let out an unforgettable guttural scream, raised its body into the air, and flew only a few metres out of danger. In the weak glare of the navigation lights, I saw that magnificent bird for a fraction of a second. I will remember it for the rest of my days. For a moment, we looked into each other's eyes. I read fear in them. I am convinced my own eyes showed the same thing. An uneasy feeling came over me. Those powerful birds are the fighters of the ocean's sky. They glide for weeks above the waves without landing. That night, it chose to float on the stormy surface, amongst the angry waves, rather than fly. My instincts told me to be on guard. It was going to be worse than I first thought.

At midnight, we were getting close to Port Stephens and the entrance to Nelson Bay. Finally, the lighthouse was visible, and we now had a visual reference to follow. We sailed towards it for a while, very happy that our misery would soon be over.

The plan was to bypass the lighthouse by steering the yacht at least a couple of miles to its right, out into the ocean, keeping well clear of the rocky shores, and only then aim for the second lighthouse inside Nelson Bay. That was what my marine navigation map showed. With the help of the portable GPS, we could finally enter the bay, keep the vessel in the middle of the entrance, make our way into the inner waters, and anchor somewhere close to shore in a wind-protected area.

But remember, there was a howling storm, and it was pitch black. The safest thing for us to do would have been to stay out in the ocean battling the weather until daylight. In our situation, the darkness was more dangerous than the gale itself. I was confident the yacht would keep us safe as long as we were in open waters. Unfortunately, Paul and Nick were badly suffering from seasickness. This debilitating motion sickness gets me sometimes too. The only explanation I could find for not having any symptoms myself was that my mind had more worrying things to focus on. And God was my witness, I was worried. I was worried about making the wrong decision. I was worried for the boat and for our lives. But it was too late to feel sorry for myself. We were in the middle of a crisis that had to be handled as best we could.

The closer we were getting to the lighthouse, the more worried I became. I didn't want to show it, and when my turn to warm up in the comfort of the cabin came, I found I couldn't rest inside anymore. No matter how cold and wet I was, I decided to stay in the cockpit next to Paul. I didn't want to take any chances. We were already pushing our luck that night. We were now at the critical part of the trip. Two pairs of eyes were better than one. I am so happy I did that.

I was in the cockpit, sitting next to Paul while he was steering the yacht. Nick was in the front cabin in bed. He was badly suffering from seasickness and, only minutes before, I had given him a couple of motion-sickness tablets to help him cope a little better. I knew his reaction to those tablets. He always became sleepy after taking them, and I felt somewhat relieved that at least he wasn't suffering as much while asleep. I was constantly looking at the GPS, the navigation map, and the distant lighthouse flashing its powerful light beams over the mad sea. I was satisfied with the distance we were keeping between our yacht and the lighthouse. According to my navigation map, the lighthouse was built right on the edge of the rocky strip of land extending into the sea. The lighthouse beams shining in our direction gave me the chance to see for a very short moment the extent of the storm around us. I could see the heavy curtains of rain falling from the heavens, the dark and impressive waves rushing towards the shore, and the streaks of water driven by the strong, gusty, howling gale. What a gloomy and worrying sight.

It was at this point that I noticed white foamy areas in the darkness of the ocean. My fears proved right when I could finally hear the roaring of breakers. That told me we shouldn't be there. We shouldn't see or hear those things. We were in shallow waters. My heart almost stopped beating. I shouted at Paul:

"– Out, Paul! … Out! … Out! … Out!"

Paul looked at me, not understanding what I meant. He didn't immediately realise something terribly wrong was about to happen.

I didn't have time for explanations. I was scared out of my mind. I took the tiller from his hands and swung the yacht out into the sea. The boat slowly turned to the right. At that very moment, she also listed 60 degrees to port in a very dangerous way. I heard the crunching sound of the keel hitting the rocks on the ocean floor. The yacht dipped bow-down and came to a stop as a result. A mountain of water coming from the front crashed onto the deck, covering us entirely.

That apocalyptic image is still recorded in my memory. In that moment, we were in mortal danger.

The massive breaker that plummeted onto the deck submerged the yacht completely, flooded the front cabin where Nick was sleeping, and smashed into the cockpit. I don't recall where Paul was at that time. When the breaker reached the cockpit, it tore me away from the tiller and threw my body into the transom safety rails. I was under the foamy water thinking those were the last moments of my life. I didn't even have time to feel scared. The chain of events came so fast it took me completely by surprise. It felt like a terrifying dream in which I was only a spectator. It couldn't be happening to me, not like that.

The next few moments felt like magic. From the frightening howling of the storm, I suddenly found myself underwater in a glowing and mesmerising world. It was quiet and tranquil. The water surrounding me was crystal clear, with a hypnotising turquoise colour. Tiny air bubbles floated everywhere, and there was peace. I was in awe. I felt weightless and free. I was convinced it was the end. I was happy.

It didn't last. A second large breaker hit the yacht. It lifted the boat from the rocky ocean floor and dropped it again violently. While the yacht was lifted, the cockpit drained, and I was once more out in the storm. I was back in my cruel reality. The gusty wind and cold rain struck my face ruthlessly, reminding me it wasn't over. It was a painful "welcome back". A strong wave of fear went through my heart. I remembered Nick, Paul, the yacht, the storm ... the rocks.

I heard myself saying:

"– Oh God! ... oh God! ..."

And God was there ... listening.

I have tears in my eyes recalling those moments. It was not over yet, it was just beginning.

I remembered that Nick had been sleeping in the front cabin. I shouted at him to get out of there and put his life jacket on. Paul rushed inside the cabin and grabbed the SOS flares and the emergency beacon. Once activated, the EPIRB would start transmitting a signal to a series of overflying satellites, which would then pinpoint our coordinates to Search and Rescue operations. I held the tiller, struggling to keep the boat facing into the waves, and realised the yacht was still scraping along the underwater reef. The sound was terrifying and heartbreaking. Wave after wave hit us mercilessly. That actually proved to be the miracle that saved our lives. Each of those furious waves lifted the yacht from the bottom. Our lifesaving luck was that the diesel engine was still running. With the propeller turning, the yacht was moving forward into deeper water. Every time the hull was lifted from the reef, we gained time. Wave by wave, metre by metre, we were getting out of danger. I could see how slowly, very slowly, the mast began to rise again. Just like my hopes that we might start floating properly once more. I was thinking and praying aloud:

"– Come on! ... come on! ... come on! ..."

A few minutes later, the yacht began to recover, and finally the mast came upright again. We were still scraping the bottom, but not as badly as before. Slowly, we reached deeper water. Crucial minutes later, we were floating freely once again. That was a miracle. We had been given a second chance. I was determined not to waste it. We were going to be safer staying with the yacht than abandoning it. That remained true as long as the boat stayed afloat.

I steered the yacht east, towards the deep sea, and began assessing the damage. Paul went back into the flooded main cabin and lifted the floor panels. It appeared we were not taking on water, the rigging was intact, and the diesel engine was still running. The front cabin was also flooded, and the entire interior of the yacht was a mess. The most important thing was that no one was hurt, and we were still afloat. I decided against entering Nelson Bay at night again. I had failed to locate the second lighthouse, which was crucial for a safe entrance, and chose the equally dreaded option of battling the raging storm from outside for the rest of the night.

I sailed the boat four to six nautical miles offshore, into the safety of deep waters, while keeping the lighthouse in sight. We had to orbit out at sea between the distant lights of Port Stephens and the first lighthouse of Nelson Bay. For the rest of the night, we circled in that area until dawn, when we would finally be able to see the dangers ahead of us.

Those were the longest, coldest and scariest four hours of my life. Later, my friend Paul admitted that too. We took turns steering the yacht in that pattern through the dark, cold, stormy and frightening night. We relied on our trusty diesel engine only. It was not safe to drift, and impossible to anchor. Nick and Paul were still suffering badly from seasickness, and the forward movement of the yacht helped slightly. Hypothermia and the 24 sleepless hours battling the weather took a heavy toll on me too. I was colder than I had ever been before. Our steering shifts were no longer than 20 minutes. I found it impossible to endure the cold caused by the wild wind and heavy rain for any longer.

Inside the yacht, Paul managed to restore some sort of normality after the flooding. He used the collapsed table and improvised a bed. Nick was still very seasick and, covered in the only sleeping bags we could find, he lay on that improvised bed trying to sleep. He couldn't help us in any way. I gave him two more seasickness tablets, which helped him cope a little better and, as a side effect, made him sleepy.

Outside, the storm was raging. The gusty wind was howling through the rigging, and the furious ocean was throwing our boat from wave to wave, leaning the mast dangerously from port to starboard. Often, the deck was covered by a breaking wave, filling the cockpit with foamy sea water and soaking us to the bone. The rain droplets whipped our faces, adding more pain to our cold and tired bodies. All I wanted at that time was to be warm, to be dry, and to go to sleep. A line from a sad war movie came to mind. I had watched it at the cinema sometime before our troubled trip. The movie was called *Unbroken*. It was a true story about an American WW2 airman who crashed into the sea and survived in a life raft for many weeks without any food or water. The main character said, "… if you can take it, you will make it." I tried to warm myself with that idea. Mind over matter. I am not convinced, but maybe it worked.

When dawn came, my spirits began rising again. What a change. I could see. I could see those large waves throwing themselves at our vessel, I could see the wild, gusty winds, I could see the rain. Most importantly, I could see in the far distance the rocky shores that had almost killed us. I could see them and not fear them. Now, I could safely stay away from them. I felt as if I had been born again. I felt great. I could face my challenges. Such a difference.

Paul asked me if I wanted a coffee. That was a great idea. Hot coffee, the ultimate spoil I could imagine in that moment. It didn't take much to forget the danger we had been in only hours before. Daylight and a hot cup of coffee.

Just after seven o'clock, I contacted Port Stephens Coast Guard by radio. I explained the situation we were in and asked for assistance.

The information given over the radio helped. We made our way into the bay, coming from the north side as directed. Our yacht entered slowly, still battling the huge waves, torrential rain, and the outgoing tide.

Once inside the safety of the bay, a group of happy dolphins joined us, swimming in front of our yacht, almost touching its hull. Their presence and playful swimming games around the boat felt like they were trying to say, "– … welcome home, guys! … we were waiting for you."

Cold, wet and very tired, we were getting close to the shore. The weather was still very bad. Yes, it was true, we were safe now, out of the fury of the large waves we had battled during the night outside the bay in the ocean, but the rain hadn't stopped, and the wind was still blowing strong, whipping our faces along with the large drops falling continuously from the heavens. The weather forecast for the following few days was as gloomy as the weather we had faced in the last 24 hours. There were warnings of major inland floods in the area and the same stormy conditions at sea. That made us rethink our plans, and we decided to leave the boat in the safety of d'Albora Marina in Nelson Bay and return home to Sydney by car.

Early in the afternoon, after the two-hour drive, we were finally in front of our house. Nick and I couldn't wait to get inside, take our wet clothes off, have a hot shower, change, and get warm. During the storm out on the ocean, I had been dreaming of that moment. Now, I was only minutes away from that much-anticipated spoil. I took my time in the shower and let the hot water warm my body. I couldn't get enough of that great feeling. Finally warm, clean of the salty water we had been soaked in, and happy to be alive, I was still in the bathroom in front of the mirror, drying myself with a soft towel.

My attention was drawn to the neck chain and the dog tags hanging on my chest. Right there next to them was also Valerie's gift, the whale bone amulet holding the Māori spell of protection. Suddenly I knew that it had performed the miracle of keeping us safe and returning all of us home. I picked it up with my fingers from where it hung on my chest, looked at it, and gently touched it with my lips. I have never taken it off my neck since.

Later that afternoon, still emotionally affected by what we had all been through, I asked my son:

"– Do you realise, Nick, that last night we were very close to finding the answer to the big question? … you know what I mean," I said, looking into his eyes. I just wanted to know his feelings about what had happened to us, hoping he wasn't traumatised by the life-threatening experience thrown at us.

Nick looked back at me with his beautiful eyes, smiled and said:

"– I know, Dad … I know. I thought about that too … but then, I knew we were going to find out together."

That was his answer.

In the corner of my eyes, two tears appeared involuntarily. I didn't expect such a deep and meaningful response. Choked by emotion, all I could say was:

"– I love you too, my boy … I love you too."

The end.

Epilogue

The next morning, we found out that we were the lucky ones.

The weather conditions had been tremendous that night. The seas were estimated at six to eight metres high, and the wind reached up to 50-knot gales. The biggest tragedy was that one human life was lost. The same storm we were in had caught an entire fleet of racing yachts competing in a regatta from Coffs Harbour to Sydney. Five yachts got into trouble, sending SOS signals, and all were rescued by Coast Guard vessels. Six sailors were washed overboard. Five were rescued, while the sixth was never found and was considered dead.

In my last phone conversation with Valerie, just before we set sail for our trip, I told her that I felt responsible for Nick and Paul, and that I was going to do my best to keep all of us safe and bring them back home.

I believe I kept my promise.

The End.

Chapter 7:
Above Us

True story

Homo sapiens, this is us, our species.

In Latin, "the wise man".

There is a question that keeps coming to my mind more often than I would like: are we really that wise? I wonder who came up with this characterisation for who we are, what we represent, and for what reason.

For thousands of years, we have considered ourselves the only spoiled children of the Universe and, my God!, we have behaved accordingly. Regrettably, from a behavioural point of view, despite our technological achievements, we have proven over and over again that we haven't significantly changed since the early years of our civilisation.

I know it is very difficult to admit this, but at the beginning of the third millennium we are still extremely selfish, inadmissibly violent, and ignorant. I am thinking about us. All we want at the end of the day is to make ourselves seen and heard. We love to impress. It seems this desire is in our genes. Suddenly, after ignoring all the material and spiritual proofs that have come to us through the centuries, we finally realise, without a doubt, that we are not alone in the Universe.

There's more. In stupor, we discover that those we might suppose to be our rivals are far more evolved than we would comfortably like to accept. In panic, we also realise that there is a good chance we could vanish without a trace, just like the thousands of plant and animal species on our planet that have disappeared because of us. For the first time in our evolution, we feel extremely vulnerable. We are no longer the ones pulling the strings. This uncomfortable fact frightens us the most, the fear of the unknown. An unknown that could be at least as bad as our own past actions in history.

We judge this new situation through the filter of our own morals, and we are afraid. So afraid that many of us refuse even to think about it or accept it as a possibility. For the same reason, some of us don't want to know at all. It is like the nightmare of the robber who dreams that he himself is robbed.

Over the years, strange things have happened in my life, so different from what we call normal, that many times, confronting myself, I reached the conclusion that they must have been the result of my imagination. Even now, when I know so much more about the whole story, I sometimes have moments when I doubt everything. It is so extraordinary. All this time, I have tried to understand it. I've tried to put the pieces together and build a full picture of this amazing puzzle, dreaming that one day I will have the entire image in front of my eyes. It is an interesting game. The more pieces I get, the bigger the picture becomes. I don't know if I will ever see that dream fulfilled, but I can tell you that so far, what is happening to us is so, so different from what we fear.

In the shortest possible way, and in chronological order, I will present to you the most significant episodes connected to this phenomenon, which happened over no more than three months. It happened in the summer of 1994, when Diane, my fiancée, and I returned from a two-month trip around the world.

Here is the story:

Not long after we returned to Australia, for reasons less important, Diane and I had a short break-up, and therefore we didn't see each other for about six weeks. At that time, I was working for a company called Avante Marine in Sydney, in a very picturesque place down on the Hawkesbury River, named Berowra Waters. My 26-foot sailing yacht was moored not far from there, and I decided to use it as a temporary residence. I thought it would be a very convenient and pleasant way to spend my solitude.

Each afternoon, at the end of my workday, I would move the boat from its mooring one or two miles downstream into a small and beautiful bay surrounded by not-too-tall but very old mountains, densely covered in eucalyptus woods. Those woods, so characteristic of Australian vegetation, were perhaps the only difference between that place and the Norwegian fjords.

Well, in this magnificent environment and in these circumstances, when I was spending most evenings and nights alone, I witnessed a chain of events that changed the course of my life forever.

During one of the first nights spent on the water, I woke up in the middle of the night feeling a strong sense of fear. It almost paralysed me. I was breathing with difficulty and, strangely, trying hard to stand up. I was not in my boat. I realised with surprise that I was not dreaming. The place was very dark and the air seemed very dense. In front of me, no more than half a metre away, a little thin humanoid-type being, fragile in appearance, allowed me to hold her hands in mine.

Because of the darkness, I couldn't distinguish her face. I cannot explain why, but I just knew she was female. I was holding her hands and, to convince myself that what was happening was real, I gently began to feel her arms. She let me do that. Unbelievable. Her arms were long and very thin. At the end of them, long, fine fingers. I noticed that the skin, if I was indeed touching skin, was fine and smooth, almost velvety. Her presence, and the fact she let me hold her hands, made me feel calm.

I sensed that I was being supported from behind by another being, taller, stronger, and without any doubt male. He helped me to stand up. I don't know why, but without feeling any pain, I somehow needed help to stand on my feet. His presence didn't scare me, but I felt weak, and I knew he was helping me. His arms were around my chest, and he was behind me to the left. He also allowed me to touch one of his arms. It felt firmer, much stronger, like ours.

Suddenly, the feeling of fear violently returns. I don't know for sure if I lost consciousness, but all I remember is waking up in my boat, exactly where I had gone to bed, in the berth of the front cabin. I was breathing heavily, and I was frightened. I felt very tired. I fell asleep again soon after, and I was awakened in the morning by my alarm clock. It was 7 am. I boiled water for coffee and, while it was cooling down, I went to the bathroom for my morning routine.

While I was washing my face and looking in the mirror, I noticed a small mark under my left eye, on the cheekbone. It was a very fine line, approximately 25 mm long, perfectly straight and uniform in the intensity of the skin inflammation. The cut or scratch was as fine as a hair. I studied it for minutes, full of curiosity. I had never had any other cut or scratch like that in my life. I couldn't decide whether what I had found was in any way connected to the experience that had happened just a few hours earlier. It was time to go to work, so I had to stop thinking about it for the moment. Despite that, I couldn't stop thinking about it all day.

At one stage, I wanted to go and see a doctor, to ask his opinion, knowing that any GP in Australia has good knowledge of most skin conditions. I was very close to doing it, but I stopped myself in time. What could I tell him? I worried he might believe I was going round the twist. In fact, all I really wanted to know was whether the scar was a scratch or a very fine burn. On the other hand, despite how important this felt to me, I thought that people with real medical problems needed him more than I did. So, I let the idea go.

Two weeks later, during another one of those nights spent alone, the story repeated itself. Suddenly, while I was sleeping, a strange vibration took over my body. Everything around me was vibrating, including myself. I was conscious of what was happening, but I couldn't react in any way. An indefinite period of time passed and I found myself standing again in a dark place, with very dense air to breathe. No more than three metres in front of me, a humanoid figure was facing me. We studied each other for a short time. I was scared. I just knew I was somehow under his power. I felt strongly affected by what I was seeing.

The being in front of me looked human. He had a short, thin body, relatively proportioned, but his head had a different shape. It was bigger than ours, rounded on top and ending in a pointed chin. His eyes were big, black, with no visible pupils, slanted in the mongoloid shape. His nose was almost non-existent, marked only by two small holes that acted as nostrils. His mouth was just a thin line without lips, giving the entire face an expression of severity. I was overcome by a strange feeling, impossible to explain. I decided to concentrate on his face. I wanted to remember every detail.

Somehow, guessing my intention, he seemed unhappy about it and, unexplainably, mentally affected my brain, stopping its normal function. It was as if the whole process of analysing and thinking was being continuously interrupted. I realised this during the short moments when my brain tried to return to normal function. It managed several times, but it was a losing battle. It was a strange and painless process.

I woke the next morning strongly affected. I remembered everything clearly. I couldn't understand why I had been stopped from remembering the details of the being's face. Again, the story repeated. While washing my face, I noticed a new scar, exactly like the one I found two weeks before. The only difference was that this one was longer, approximately 35 mm, on the left cheek again but lower, closer to the jaw. Could this be another coincidence? It seemed almost impossible.

One week later, during the night, I woke up in fear and panic. I found myself in a dark environment. I was lying horizontally on something I couldn't describe because of the darkness. I sensed the presence of other people around me. I was talking, probably answering questions I couldn't remember. What I did remember was that I was very scared. Suddenly, from the dark, somebody came closer. This time I was petrified. I tried desperately to stand up but I couldn't move. All I could move was my head. I tried as hard as I could, forcing all my muscles and using all my energy, without any success. I was very close to a nervous breakdown.

In that moment, right in front of my eyes, bright electrical discharges appeared several times, accompanied by sound. They seemed to come from a wand made of some unknown translucent material. The wand was approximately 400 mm long and was held very close to my face by someone I couldn't see. Instantly, my attention was drawn to those shiny light sparks in front of me. It was exactly the same process that affected my brain's normal function as the one I described before. It took several seconds of hard concentration to maintain my lucidity, but in the end, I lost consciousness.

I came around after an indefinite amount of time. I was in the same place, seated on a kind of bed, quite high off the floor. My body was in a sitting position with my hands behind my back. In the dark room, four or five silhouettes looked busy doing something I couldn't identify. Suddenly, one of them came closer. For some reason, I didn't get scared. It came so close that I felt strangely uncomfortable. A young and pretty woman with a human appearance stopped only a few centimetres away. Being so close, I could distinguish her face and upper body very clearly. She was very feminine, with short hair, warm eyes, and a discreet smile. She addressed me directly, without introduction, as if we were old friends:

"– It is time for me to go back home, where I came from," she said, her voice calm, with a slight regret in it.

"– I came to tell you goodbye."

"– Where did you come from?" I asked.

"– Our home is in the Lyre Constellation," she answered. She told me the name of the planet too, but because I had never heard the name before, I forgot it instantly. It wasn't important for me at that moment to try to memorise it. I was far too overwhelmed by what was happening.

In the morning, when I woke up, I remembered everything clearly. I looked curiously for the scar. It wasn't on the left cheek. It wasn't on the right cheek either. Amazed, I found it on the inner part of my left forearm, close to the elbow, where the skin is finer. The same strange night event, the same coincidence. Approximately 40 mm long, with the same characteristics as the other two. The third time, after a night of strange experiences, I discovered the same kind of unusual scars inscribed on my body.

And the story doesn't end here. After six weeks of solitude, Diane rang me at work. The reason was some photos taken during the holiday we had spent together, she wanted me to have them.

It was time for reconciliation. This took place on a Thursday evening on my yacht, with a wonderful seafood dinner and champagne. We had a lot to talk about, and eventually, we realised that time had flown and it was late. It was too late for Diane to return to her apartment, so I invited her to stay on the yacht with me until the following morning, when we both had to go to work.

We finally fell asleep at midnight. Sometime later that night, I woke suddenly. Something wasn't right. I was surprised to find Diane awake too. Spending so many days and nights on the yacht, I had learned how to involuntarily perceive a lot of signs which could indicate that something was out of the ordinary, the way the yacht moved on the waves, the sound of the rigging, the vibration of the engine, the sounds of the birds and other marine life. Generally speaking, almost everything could bring suspicion and needed attention.

This time was something else. We were awakened in the middle of the night by a strong mechanical noise, which seemed to be coming from the deck above us. For longer than three minutes, we could hear that strange noise. With reasonable approximation, it sounded like a ball made of metal chains, rolling very fast across the entire deck and the cabin ceiling. I analysed all the possibilities I could think of. I concluded that it was impossible for the yacht itself to make the noise. That night there was no wind or waves, and the boat was floating still in perfectly calm water. The anchor and its heavy chain, 8 metres long, was lying sunken in the mud on the river bottom. Nothing on the deck was loose, nothing that could produce that noise. The boat didn't move at all.

For a moment, I considered the possibility that a nocturnal animal, like a big rat or an otter, had swum from the shore to the boat, climbed the anchor line, and run across the deck with its claws searching for food. Perhaps it could produce a noise like that. It was close, but hard to believe that something like that could sound so loud and metallic, while giving the impression of such rapid movement.

I was sleepy and confused. It was the first time I had witnessed this kind of phenomenon. I decided to go outside to see what was happening. Halfway from the bed to the exit hatch, the noise stopped and never repeated that night again.

The following morning, we got up early. Sleepy, I rushed to start the engine, pull up the anchor, and move the yacht back to its mooring. Over time, I got used to checking all the instruments on the electric board after starting the engine, especially those that monitor its operation. Three were more important: the oil pressure gauge, the alternator voltage gauge, and the current gauge, which monitors the electric current in the system.

Following routine, I checked each instrument separately. With suspicion and confusion, my gaze stopped on the current gauge. The indicator needle was stuck all the way to the right, showing a measurement far higher than the maximum the gauge was designed to measure. The maximum limit shown on the screen was 50 amps. The needle had been forced and stuck at over 150 amps. It had never happened before. Yet, the engine and the electric system continued to function perfectly. Could this be a fourth coincidence?

I remembered reading that in the majority of UFO landings or close-range sightings, there were also reports of strong magnetic disturbances. It is well known from the laws of physics, more precisely, from the law of electromagnetic induction, that a variation in a magnetic field induces a current in an electrical circuit, directly proportional to the intensity and speed of the variation of the magnetic field.

I couldn't help thinking that it was possible my current gauge had been affected by a very intense current induced in the engine's electrical circuit by a strong magnetic field nearby, generated by the metallic object which rolled on the deck of my boat and woke us that night. It was not the time to reach any conclusions; the story wasn't finished yet.

Despite being officially back together, Diane and I decided to take things slowly. We saw each other two or three times a week, generally at her place, where we would have dinner and spend unforgettable moments together. On weekends, we spent more time with our own children, Diane with her son, and I with my daughter, Lisa.

I remember that on one of those weekends, as I had promised Lisa for a long time, we went to visit Taronga Zoo in Sydney. We spent most of the day there. Lisa dragged me from one enclosure to another, ensuring we didn't miss any creature, big or small. I had seen most of them before, so everything was for her.

However, when we reached the enclosure of the giant Galapagos tortoises, it was different. The minute I saw them, I was captivated by the heads of those creatures. Their grey, wrinkled skin, the absence of ears and hair, the large black eyes, the Mongoloid look, the almost nonexistent noses marked by two small holes, and mouths that were only thin lines without lips, all gave them a severe look. What an extraordinary likeness!

The only differences were the shape of their heads and the size of their mouths. I watched them fascinated, asking myself if it was really possible that I, an average human being, had been privileged enough to meet those nocturnal beings that mysteriously kept appearing in my life at night. It was strange that the closest connection I had with them evoked such a powerful reaction in me. I asked myself if all of it was a product of my imagination, generating such confusion. The truth, only God knew.

The surprises don't end here. Taronga Zoo has one of the biggest chimpanzee colonies living in semi-captivity in the world. Almost 30 individuals of all ages, from babies to the very old, are kept in an area of approximately one square kilometre, developed very close to their natural habitat. Once we were there, face to face with our less-advantaged-by-chance relatives, I was overcome by thoughts. This time, I was strongly affected by our similarity. I am not referring only to the physical likeness; I am talking about all aspects. We look at them and we see ourselves. Same gestures, same expressions, same manifestations.

I continue my reflections. What sincere explanation could we possibly have for taking the most precious gift of a living being, their freedom, and pushing them together in an enclosure surrounded by barbed wire? They were born free. The true answer is that we don't have such a right. We have an excuse, though. The only excuse we could use is… to study them.

I am shaking. Is it possible that the same thing could, did, or is happening to us? If yes… by whom? I am frozen. By Them! Oh God! Maybe I am not far from the truth. It is logical and, above all, not impossible. My thoughts fly even further. Is it possible that this Blue Planet could, to some extent, be their zoo? Very probable. If yes, is it possible that even They themselves were once the study subjects of someone else… and that Someone else had their turn as well? In other words, we study each other in the net of space and time, and so the circle is closed.

I am back to reality. It was time to go home.

No more than two or three days after this episode, I was on my yacht in the afternoon, preparing to go and meet Diane at her apartment. I was in the little bathroom, half undressed, washing. Suddenly, I looked in the mirror and saw something on my right forearm. I couldn't believe what I was seeing. Almost in the same position as my last mark, on my right arm where the skin is finer, I had a similar type of scar. This time, it was a perfect circle. I had no visions and I was perfectly lucid. Clear and distinct, with amazing precision, a circle approximately 25 mm in diameter was undeniably drawn there. The same thing: a fine red line, thin as hair, perfectly continuous and uniform, was visible without any doubt.

I am not exaggerating. I am not making this up. All I want is to give you a chance to judge these facts for yourselves and, in the end, reach your own conclusions.

Back to the story.

At that moment, I didn't know what to do. There was no way this scar could have been self-inflicted, not in that shape or form. It was a perfect circle. I didn't have the slightest memory of any strange experience, and that made it a bit scary. I remembered only one link between me and that circle on my arm: the result of my reflections at the Zoo the previous weekend. Could it be possible that in this way, Somebody was admitting that I was not far from the truth? Could it also be possible that those extraordinary beings are able to read and record my thoughts from a distance? That was the only explanation I could logically find.

I am still in the yacht's bathroom, thinking. It is so extraordinary, I can hardly admit it to myself. I check it several times to see if the scar is still there. I am worried that it could disappear at any moment. Everything was possible. It was late and Diane was waiting for me. I drove in a daze, disobeying the traffic rules, and amazingly reached my destination in one piece. I rang the bell and, when the apartment door opened, Diane knew from the expression on my face that something had happened. She asked me what.

Without answering, I rolled up the sleeve of my shirt. Just looking at my arm, Diane understood.

I had an idea. I asked Diane to fetch the camera. I took the camera and installed a new film. It was a new Polaroid, totally automatic. As usual with a new film, I wound it to the starting position. It worked perfectly, including the flash. Diane took two pictures of my arm and I took one. Everything worked normally.

The following weekend, as usual, I had Lisa. I don't remember exactly what we did during the day, but I do remember that one evening that weekend, I used the same camera inside my boat, taking a few shots with my daughter while she was drawing.

The next weekend, I believe she was invited to a birthday party for one of her school friends, and because of that we didn't see each other. I invited Diane to come with me on a sailing trip down the Hawkesbury River. During this trip, I anchored the yacht in a small and very picturesque bay, surrounded by mountains. We wanted to stretch our legs, so we decided to go to shore. We left the yacht anchored and, using the little dinghy, rowed to land.

Once we reached the shore, we saw a mountain cliff not too far away, roughly 100 feet above sea level. Curious about the view from up there, we climbed until we reached it. We weren't disappointed. Australia was showing off one of its beauties. We had the camera with us and took advantage of that. The pictures showed the bay below, the anchored yacht waiting for us, the surrounding shores, and the sky covered with only a few white, fluffy, good-weather clouds. It was beautiful.

Excited by that amazing panorama, I took a few more pictures until I had finished the film. I was so impatient to have it developed that I rewound the film right there on the cliff.

Well, something happened which took me by surprise and beyond my imagination. Once the film unwound, somewhere inside the automatic camera I could hear strange noises and feel internal mechanical movements. Diane witnessed this too. I was just holding the camera without touching any buttons. I shook the camera lightly, hoping it might stop. No effect. The strange sounds and internal movements continued for at least 30 seconds. Suddenly they stopped. I rushed to take the film out to check it. Everything appeared to be okay. It was the film containing the photos of the circle on my arm, the pictures taken with Lisa inside the yacht, and the ones taken recently from the cliff.

The next afternoon after work, I rushed to get the film developed. In one hour, the pictures were ready. I was a bit nervous when the young shop assistant handed me the envelope with the photos and negatives. Impatiently, I paid her and took the pictures out. I felt better for a moment when I saw that all the photos so far were good. Then I noticed that the photos with the circle mark on my arm were missing. I was confused and ready to protest. Just before doing so, I opened the envelope again and took out the negatives. My hands were shaking.

Unbelievable.

The first three frames, the ones with the circle mark on my arm, were blank.

Another coincidence?

Becomes hard to believe. For some unknown reason, I have been denied the opportunity to have those photos. My frustration increases day by day. I try to understand the logic or the meaning of what is happening to me. I know that I can't find an answer by myself. I don't think anybody can realise how frustrating that is. We are not talking about a normal thing. I mentioned it before: it is not us pulling the strings anymore. I tried everything logically possible. I bought books on this subject. After reading them, I soon understood that the answer didn't lie there. The majority of the books narrated only other people's experiences. They were only guesses. I met people who study this phenomenon individually or in organised research groups. Same story. I found out that I knew more than them.

As a last resort, I had several hypnotic regression sessions. This method proved to be the most fruitful. Sadly, even this technique is not unbeatable. Most of my memories were so strongly hidden in my subconscious that reaching them required good knowledge and professionalism in the hypnotic field. During this time I met three different hypnotherapists. Two of them managed to unveil the natural barrier of the brain's self-protection against the intense and traumatic experiences this phenomenon exposes its subjects to. The third one tried a new method which unfortunately didn't work in my case.

I was very close to acccpting what Diane tried to convince me of, that "no matter how hard I was fighting for an answer, I will never have it."

Well, if I couldn't find an explanation for this conundrum in a normal way, I decided to directly ask Them.

One would say that I had lost my mind. Initially, I thought that too. After a while though, I told myself that this idea was not as silly as it sounded. I had nothing to lose. During that period, I started to spend two or three nights a week with Diane in her apartment. Usually after work, I went to the yacht, changed my clothes, and around six o'clock in the evening I went to see her.

One of those afternoons, while I was still on my boat, I had an idea. On an A4 white piece of paper, with a black texter, I drew a rectangular border roughly 150 mm long and 100 mm high. Inside that rectangular shape, I drew on two levels all the skin marks I had imprinted on my body in the order I found them, and proportional to their original sizes. The first sign on the top level was a triangle I discovered printed on my left cheek under the eye. It appeared while I was spending a few nights on my yacht on a different occasion, two years earlier. The next ones were the straight marks. The last sign was the circle. With it, I ended up in the middle of the rectangle on the second level. From the circle, I drew a short line of dots ending with a horizontal arrow. Outside the rectangular shape containing the symbols of the skin marks, in the top right corner, I drew a question mark.

After I finished, I thought about this attempt and smiled. It felt childish even to me, the author, but even so, I went ahead with it.

I will try to explain what was going through my mind when I drew this diagram. The rectangular shape represented the whole story I was implicated in. The inside signs represented the shape of the marks imprinted on my skin, and being inside the rectangular shape reiterated that I connected with this phenomenon. The line of dots followed by the horizontal arrow was imagined as representing the direction this phenomenon was going to take regarding my person. The question mark in the top right corner represented just that, puzzle, curiosity, an invitation for explanation.

And so, I continued the game. I set the piece of paper with the drawn diagram, together with the black texter, on the collapsible navigation table in the main cabin of the yacht. Mentally, I formulated an invitation to an answer, and in the end, I left the boat, going to meet Diane at her apartment for dinner. I felt somehow ashamed of myself for what I had just done. It looked childish and senseless. I had almost forgotten this juvenile action when, on the third day, I was in the boat changing my clothes and involuntarily looked at the piece of paper left on the navigation table.

The answer was there! I couldn't believe my eyes. Amazed, I discovered that I had been answered in the same manner. In fact, the answer contained my own drawing, my own thoughts. It was short, clear, unmistakable. It was a reformulation of my own question. On the rectangular border, in the place where the horizontal arrow was pointing, the borderline had been interrupted. In that area, thc black texter ink had disappeared. In this way, the diagram changed its meaning. In other words, the answer was: "… the story is not finished! …"

I believe it is time now to say: " … I rest my case! …"

You give the verdict!

Post Scriptum

The story didn't finish indeed. It continues with the same frequency and in the same way. Sometimes, I have the privilege to be allowed to remember small fragments of my own experiences. I understand that there is a good reason for it and I hope that one day, I will be told what it is.

After one of my recent events, I noticed that the yacht's portable television stopped working. I had to have it fixed. The repair company did that and sent me the bill with a comment attached to it:

" … this type of fault is extremely uncommon and was caused by a very strong magnetic interference … "

Epilogue

This is the story of only three specific months. Since then, many other incidents took place and each one added its own detail to the big picture. Looks like I am building a mysterious and surprising puzzle with unknown borders.

After so many years of accumulation, the big questions were still there:

"Who are they?

Where do they come from?

What do they want?"

Unexpectedly, the best answer to date came from my six-year-old daughter, Lisa. It happened on a Sunday night, in the car, while I was driving her back to her mother's house after a weekend spent together. Lisa was a pretty, happy, healthy and clever six-year-old girl. I loved her then at least as much as I love her now. That evening, as usual, she was sitting in the rear seat of the car and happily chitchatting with me about everything and everybody. She was a chatterbox that night and, preoccupied with my driving, I was only half paying attention to what she was saying.

"You know daddy, those *Shapes* came in my room last night again," she said, suddenly changing the subject.

My heart stopped for a moment. She had never talked about anything like that before. I had never heard her mention the *Shapes*. In that moment, I paid full attention. I didn't know where the conversation was going, but I had an idea what she meant. I knew what she meant. I turned the radio off and, a few moments later, when my surprise let me speak, I asked:

"What do you mean, Lisa? … what Shapes are you talking about?"

I looked in the rear-vision mirror to see her face. She was smiling in complicity. She was waiting for my reaction. She gave me the impression she was doing a naughty thing by talking about it, something she shouldn't really do.

"You know daddy, *the Shapes*. They do come in my room in the night from time to time," she added. Because she had never mentioned this to me before, I wanted to find out more without making her uncomfortable talking about it. She didn't look scared.

"No Lisa, I don't know. What do they do in your room? Do they talk to you? Do they sing to you? ... please tell me."

She laughed.

"Noooo... daddy, don't be silly. They don't talk and they don't sing to me. They have different colours, and they move around in the room and they form different shapes, and all of these make me feel good. One of them has a Chinese face."

(The dark slanted eyes, I believe, is what she meant.)

I was in shock. I could hardly believe my ears. Such an unexpected surprise. She sounded serious and convincing. A few more questions came to my mind but I didn't want to confuse her. She was only six years old. I asked instead:

"Who are they, Lisa?

Where do they come from?

What do they want?"

Her answer came a moment later, in one simple phrase. It looked like she didn't even have to think about it. It felt as though the answer was already there in her mind, waiting to be released. I will remember it for the rest of my life. These are her very words:

"They are foreign people which came here from a different country in a plane and they just study us, silently into the night …"

The End.

By Victor Liviu Pufulescu